L. B. GREE~~~~

Sherlock Holmes and the Thistle of Scotland

SIMON AND SCHUSTER
New York London Toronto Sydney Tokyo

Grateful Acknowledgment to Dame Jane Conan Doyle for permission to use the Sherlock Holmes characters created by Sir Arthur Conan Doyle

SIMON & SCHUSTER
Rockefeller Center
1230 Avenue of the Americas
New York, New York 10020

SIMON & SCHUSTER and colophon are trademarks
of Simon & Schuster Inc.

Designed by Deirdre C. Amthor.

Manufactured in the United States of America

10 9 8 7 6 5 4 3 2 1

Library of Congress Catalog-in-Publication Data

Greenwood, L.B.
Sherlock Holmes and the Thistle of Scotland / L.B. Greenwood.
p.   cm.
I. Holmes, Sherlock (Fictitious character)—Fiction.   I. Title.
PS3557.R3975s56 1989 89-36201
813'.54—dc20   CIP

ISBN 0-7432-0552-9

To W. T. G. with love and gratitude

To myriad lovers of detective fiction, 1887 will forever be the vintage year: the first appearance in print of Sherlock Holmes. That a century later the name of literature's greatest investigator is still as powerful as ever proves the creative genius of Sir Arthur Conan Doyle.

Chapter I

A Chequered Delight
—Charles Dibdin,
Saturday Night at Sea

During my service as an army medical officer in India, I had the double misfortune of first being wounded and then contracting a debilitating fever. Though by the time I had returned home and bought a practice in London, I felt fit enough, when I became seriously overtired I was forcefully reminded of the youthful energies that had been sacrificed to the glories of empire. At such times I would end my day as soon as possible and turn my weary steps toward home. There my understanding wife would tuck a rug around my legs and sit beside me with the evening paper, reading aloud any items that she thought would interest my flagging spirits. Thus it was that in the summer of 1890 I first heard of the Thistle of Scotland.

This historic piece of jewellery had been one of the betrothal gifts of Lord Darnley to Mary Queen of Scots. In compliment to her native country, a huge facet-cut amethyst had been set at the head of a delicate silver thistle, and the whole shaped into a clip for her hair. The queen had been wearing the ornament at the time of her capture, and had used it to reward the young laird who had helped her escape from Lochleven. Ever since, the Thistle of Scotland had been a prized heirloom among the ladies of his house.

What had now brought this royal jewel to the attention of the London editors was the tragedy that had engulfed its present owner, the elderly Lady Helen Picton of Sterling. Her whole family had recently been lost in a yachting accident off the Firth of Forth, and under this terrible blow Lady Picton herself was said to be near death. The question of who would inherit the historic piece, valued by Gerrard's at four thousand pounds, was thus arousing considerable speculation.

I suppose this little story stayed in my mind because a doctor sees so much drear loss that has not a tinge of romance about it. Certainly when near the end of September Mary read out to me the announcement of the death of Lady Picton and the inheritance of the Thistle of Scotland by her goddaughter, Lady Caroline Mowbray, I remembered it and was interested when I again heard these names.

This occurred in late October, and I had dined at Boodle's, the guest of a grateful patient. After finishing supper with the club's justly famous orange fool, we repaired to the smoking room for cigars and some excellent brandy. The weather was unseasonably cold, my elderly host was soon dozing, and I, glad enough to sit quietly by the fire, found myself idly listening to the talk of four men sitting nearby.

"I hear Mowbray has made a marriage for Lady Caroline," a grey-haired man observed.

"So I understand," a second replied, with a faint expression of distaste. "To that chap who's taken the corporation in so shockingly on those Ludgate Hill properties."

"Adolphus Stanley?" the third asked in obvious surprise, then quickly answered himself. "Of course: the Thistle of Scotland—that's what's made the match."

"Didn't know Dolph Stanley ever invested in jewels," the second commented.

"He doesn't, but, according to the talk on 'Change, he's used the last of his ready cash to take up the Ludgate Hill options. The only possession he's got to raise interest-free money on being himself, he approached Mowbray's lawyer, and the deal was made."

"I'm surprised a City chap was even aware of Lady Caroline's inheritance," the first speaker observed, rather disapprovingly. "I only heard it from Mowbray himself, at our club."

"Oh, the Dolph Stanleys of the world always know whatever will benefit them," the second replied drily.

"So Lady Caroline's inheritance is to be turned into cash and given to Stanley as her dowry, he no doubt settling the property on her? Well, if the jewel turns up the right sum—"

"Apparently it's already been sold, for five thousand pounds."

"*Five* thousand! Why, the papers said the value was four, didn't they? Quoting Gerrard's too."

"That American chap who's over here with those railroad bonds wasn't taking any chance of being overbid. He wants to take the Thistle of Scotland home for his wife."

"Stanley knew of the American, no doubt?"

"Naturally."

———

"Doesn't seem as if Lady Caroline receives much from the whole thing," the fourth and youngest of the group spoke for the first time. "Here she's had the amazing luck to inherit a historic jewel, and now she isn't going to be allowed to keep it."

"It's give up the stone or give up the marriage," the first member replied with a shrug, "so no doubt Lady Caroline is happy enough. I know she was presented the same year as my daughter," he added as if this quite clinched the matter, "and Viola has two little ones of her own now."

"That means more to a woman than amethysts, no matter how historic," the second speaker concurred. This brought a general murmur of agreement, though I noticed that the youngest member looked dubious and said nothing. When I arrived home, I reported the whole conversation to Mary and asked her opinion. Would Lady Caroline be happy to exchange her newly inherited jewel for a husband, a husband, too, from the City?

"I suppose she must be," my wife replied, reaching for the newspaper, "for here is the announcement of the coming marriage of Lady Caroline Mowbray, only daughter of Earl and Countess Mowbray of Lambeth, to Mr. Adolphus Merriweather Stanley, to take place at the church of St. George the Martyr on a date near the middle of November."

"Why, that's little more than a fortnight from now!" I exclaimed. "Not much time for preparations, is there?"

"I suppose the wedding is to be a very quiet one," my wife replied, "though the paper does say that Lady Caroline is going to wear the clip for the service. The noted gemmologist, Mr. Arthur Manning of Gerrard's, will deliver the famous Thistle of Scotland to Mowbray House just prior to the family's leaving for the church, and will collect it later that same day.' They certainly aren't taking any chances, are they?"

"Hardly surprising when five thousand pounds are at stake, not to mention the girl's marriage," I replied, picking up the latest *Lancet.* I was deep in an article by Almroth Wright on the pathology of war wounds, a topic of considerable interest to me, when I again became conscious of my wife's voice.

"I wonder," she was saying, "if Lady Caroline *is* happy, marrying a man willing to have her merely because she's inherited a valuable jewel. It seems such a terribly business-like way of getting married, doesn't it?"

"Not the way *we* married, certainly," I agreed, smiling.

Mary, though, wasn't thinking of us; her sympathetic heart was concerned with the welfare of the unknown Lady Caroline. "I wonder," she repeated thoughtfully, "what she's like?"

"My dear," I replied, returning to my medical journal, "that is something we will never know."

There I had certainly drawn an incorrect conclusion.

Before the end of that chilly October Sherlock Holmes and I went to the Lyceum to see Henry Irving and Ellen Terry in their celebrated presentation of *Macbeth.* Such shared evenings were infrequent for us now, for my own commitments and the idiosyncratic nature of Holmes's habits meant that we were seldom together. Perhaps for that reason we were the more reluctant to let the evening end, and so, instead of waiting under the theatre's stately pillared portico for a cab, we had stepped around to the Tivoli for a buffet supper, and were now braving the falling temperature to stroll along the Strand, still talking.

To be more accurate, we were engaged in one of our lively disputes, this time on the performance we had just attended. Holmes approved of Irving's interpretation, which portrayed Macbeth as guilty from the outset; I felt this reduced a tragic figure to an emotional and uninteresting weakling. Miss Terry's reading of Lady Macbeth I found a moving departure from the usual stormy presentation, and her beetlewing dress the vision of iridescent beauty that the newspapers had promised; Holmes thought her both insipid and sentimental and acidly observed that, if her green gown should set a fashion, naturalists would have to look to their collections.

As well, Holmes went on, leading us down a deserted by-street, the management's choice of entr'acte entertainment was deplorable. "If you are fortunate enough to have music by Sullivan for the performance," Holmes complained, his high voice becoming decidedly strident, "why add anything?"

"I enjoyed the contrast," I countered.

"Indeed? Even that tenor?" Holmes struck a ridiculous attitude, admittedly all too like that of the disparaged singer, and warbled in falsetto, "'The moon on the ocean was disarmed by a ripple, Affording a chequered delight. . . ' Precisely what is a chequered delight? Some new candy from Constantinople, perhaps?"

As if in response to this sarcastic query, a shout of laughter and a quick scamper of feet came from somewhere behind us. Turning, we saw two male figures spring gaily out of a narrow alley-way into the yellowish light of a street lamp nearby. One was a tall, broad-shouldered man, dressed in evening clothes topped by a stylish opera cloak and moving with the sinuous grace of prime physical condition.

His companion was different in every way, much slighter and shorter, sporting a shabby cloth-cap, brownish tweed jacket, and a pair of the most astoundingly loud check trousers that I have ever seen.

As they rounded the corner of the alley, the lad (for he seemed no more) suddenly stumbled and would have fallen had it not been for the big man's quick grasp. For some reason this slight mishap brought forth a fresh burst of merriment, and the young fellow, keeping a hold of his companion's hands, began an impromptu dance around him, stamping his patched boots and making much laughing play with his chequered legs.

A cab could be heard approaching from Charing Cross; the well-dressed stranger raised his fingers to his mouth and, with a piercing whistle, brought the hansom cantering smartly in our direction. Before it had completely stopped, the man had boosted his young companion inside with an upward push on the rear, and, springing lightly aboard himself, his cape swinging with an arrogant flourish around him, he half-turned his head toward our shadowed corner. We had a fleeting glimpse of white teeth gleaming under a dark moustache, of black eyes devilishly bright, before the apron shut and the disappearing cab blended into the inky night.

"Well!" I rather pointlessly exclaimed, looking about me and startled to find nothing familiar. "Where on earth are we, Holmes?"

Holmes was gazing across at the alley entrance, a slight frown creasing his lean face. "Lost already? What a creature of the tried and true paths you are, Doctor. We're on Sinuleron Street, and that man in the opera cape was Carrington Fitzgerald. You've heard of him?"

"I should think half England has heard of him," I

said, "not to mention most of Ireland," for Fitzgerald was a scion of one of County Tyrone's leading families and, while at school and at university, had been the darling of all. The untimely death of his father, however, had led to a dozen years of such fast living that, his estate in ruins and his reputation black, he had disappeared into the outposts of the empire. From there occasional tales of his mad exploits—in which, to give him his due, bravery and endurance often featured as prominently as scandalous and even illegal behaviour—at times drifted back to his homeland. "I didn't know he had returned to London. Nor," I added with disgust, "that his taste for late-hour amusement ever ran to boys."

"Nor I, quite the reverse. He must have some other game afoot tonight. As for his presence in London, Lord Dunsmere is dying in Dublin, so they say, and refusing to see the nephew who has so disgraced the family name. Accordingly Fitzgerald waits here, with a legion of creditors at his back. The hopes of neither can be very high, though Fitzgerald hardly seems down-hearted. As for that boy..." Holmes paused, and his frown deepened.

A second cab had appeared at the end of the short street, and I, who had had a long day, stepped out into the lamplight and raised my stick. "Possibly the presence of that lad in the check trousers was mere chance and quite innocent."

"Carr Fitzgerald is usually the manipulator of chance," Holmes replied, "and it is years since any of his activities could accurately be called innocent."

Our cab pulled up, I climbed in, but Holmes did not immediately follow. When I leaned out to see what was keeping him, I found him walking slowly back toward the entrance, bent double and staring down at the pavement.

"Whatever are you looking for?" I called.

He made no answer until he himself had at last entered the cab, and then his reply made little sense to me. "I was looking for an explanation as to why that young chap in the check trousers stumbled."

"And did you find one?"

"I did not."

"I should think a bottle of wine consumed at supper holds the answer," I said. "The lad is no doubt unused to such luxury and over-indulged."

"Yet he stepped out neatly and briskly enough in that little dance, didn't he?"

I agreed, though without interest. That this brief incident would have any connection with one of Holmes's most intriguing cases was an idea then very far from my thoughts.

Chapter II

And in my lady's chamber
—*Goosey, Goosey, Gander*

The cold weather of late October worsened until to be outdoors at all became a burden. When, near the middle of November, I foresaw a quiet Sunday, Mary and I were only too glad to plan to stay by our own fire. Hardly had we settled down after lunch, however, when the crisp beat of a fast-trotting horse and the rattle of an equally fast-moving hansom threatened our warm sanctuary.

I put down my paper, Mary lowered her embroidery, and, as the noise abruptly ceased at our gate, we exchanged a look of dreary anticipation. Sure enough, our bell sounded, and, as the girl went to answer it, I heaved myself to my feet. Before I reached the door, it was unceremoniously flung wide, and there, hat and stick still in his gloved hands, stood Sherlock Holmes.

"I beg your pardon for this intrusion, Mrs. Watson," he began with his unfailing courtesy. "No, I won't sit down, for I must be on my way very shortly.

I have been called out on a case that really promises so well that I felt I had to see if Watson would care to accompany me. Did you happen to notice any of the newspaper accounts last summer of the amethyst hair clip known as the Thistle of Scotland?"

"We did," my wife replied in obvious surprise. As for me, I was already on my way into the hall for my coat.

"Then you probably know that the daughter of the Earl of Mowbray inherited it from her godmother. The jewel from the clip has now disappeared."

"Stolen?" Mary cried, her work dropping from her fingers.

"That is certainly the inference, Mrs. Watson."

"But I understood the clip was to be kept at Gerrard's," I protested from the doorway, winding a scarf around my neck, "until the day of the wedding. Why, that's today!"

"Quite right, Watson, and according to the frantic note I have just received from Countess Mowbray, the amethyst has somehow vanished from Lady Caroline's hair while she was sitting at her wedding breakfast, in her father's house and in full view of twenty assembled people. So if you'll forgive my absconding with your husband, Mrs. Watson . . ."

"*I* won't forgive him if he doesn't go," my wife replied with a smile, "for I feel a particular interest in Lady Caroline. Mind you bring me all the details, John."

Within minutes Holmes and I were bowling rapidly along through the pale sunlight of a sharp autumn day.

"I really know nothing of the Mowbray family," I remarked as we turned down Edgeware Road, "though their name seems somewhat familiar."

"That is probably a faint echo from some history

master of your youth, for the Mowbrays were briefly important as staunch supporters of Henry the Eighth. They received the land on which Mowbray House still stands, not far from Lambeth Palace, and also an estate in Kent as part of their reward. Unfortunately they have never been prominent since, and are reported to be living in near poverty amid the ruins of their former greatness."

"The papers referred to Lady Caroline as the only daughter. There are sons?"

"Only Eustace, two years older than Lady Caroline and by all accounts a nonentity. The estate is of course entailed upon him, though I'm afraid it is a white elephant of an inheritance."

"Then perhaps Lady Caroline was wise after all to accept the marriage," I commented, and repeated what I had overheard at Boodle's.

"That suggests that the bride is a more practical young woman than many of her age and sex," Holmes observed with satisfaction, "which augurs well for the process of our investigation. Information given under the stress of hysteria is a trial to collect and seldom reliable."

"How did Countess Mowbray come to send for you?" I asked, as we started across Vauxhall Bridge.

"She is a family connection of Mrs. Agnes Marshall."

"The Blueschool Charity Case." I nodded my understanding. "Was Mrs. Marshall a guest at the breakfast?"

"She was, yes."

"Then you should have at least one very reliable witness," I observed, remembering that vigorous lady's sharp eyes and quick intelligence. The sound of bells calling for evensong at some old-fashioned church made me consult my watch. "If the theft occurred at the breakfast, Holmes, and it is now nearly four..."

"I know. Almost undoubtedly the police will have been on the scene for several hours, and that is never promising. Still, remember the motto of the firm: we can but try."

We turned left off Kennington Lane and then left again on Black Prince Road, to begin a complicated meander through small streets unknown to me, to whom the London south of the Thames was little familiar. What was most obvious about the area was that it was in the midst of change: the railroad expansion for Waterloo Station and the clearing done for the Albert Embankment had accelerated a process that the disastrous fires earlier in the century had started.

Much of the new was good—the closed shops looked prosperous, the streets were clean, and the occasional bank interjected a note of commercial solidity—and some was even artistic: I looked with particular satisfaction toward the Palladian structure of St. Thomas's Hospital. Yet there was that raw unease to the landscape that lasts until time has made neighbours of merely adjacent buildings, and, as we rounded the Archbishop's Park, I wondered what Mowbray House would be like. I soon knew.

Once, no doubt, the town residence of the Mowbrays had been set in extensive grounds that had made a fitting background for the sixteenth-century building; the forced economies of the intervening years had ruined the appearance of both. Scarcely half a neglected acre remained of the gardens, these cut off from Dean Street by a wandering crescent lined with overgrown yew. The house was four stories of gauged brick, with a hipped roof sprouting chimney-pots like dirty mushrooms, fronted by three

21

tiers of mullioned windows and with the entrance formed by an excrescence of grey stone with two fluted Ionic columns supporting a segmented pediment.

"What is the fee?" Holmes had opened the slot in the roof to call up to our driver. "Five-and-three? Dear me! I foresee that this case is going to cost a fortune in cab fares. Odd that Lady Caroline was married at St. George's; one would have expected the wedding to have been at some nearer church—we must have passed at least three." Holmes climbed out and surveyed Mowbray House. "It's as well that we have the countess's sanction to call. Our immediate welcome doesn't appear warm, does it?"

By this stage in his career, Holmes was considered by the majority of London policemen to be their best friend at all times. A few, however, jealously protective of their own prerogatives, never could view his presence kindly, and it was one of this latter species who stood with broad back against the panelled door and pugnacious chin set firmly into the high stock collar of his uniform. Fortunately the countess's note could not be dismissed, and we were grudgingly permitted to use the heavy brass knocker.

The door was opened, though none too promptly, by the butler, a thin, grey-haired man whose black suit had more than a hint of rust about it and whose manner was much harassed. He led us across a handsome though bare hall into the library, a large square room very scantily furnished. Even those few items—a desk, a settee, and a couple of chairs, all huddled together in front of the majestic marble hearth—were shabby, and the solid-oak shelves lining the walls from floor to ceiling were far less than a quarter full of unmatched volumes, all looking either untouched or tattered. The butler lingered to apologize for the necessity of using this chamber, explaining that the police were still in possession of both the drawing- and the dining-rooms.

"In fact, sir," he added bitterly, "I would hardly be wrong to say they're in possession of the whole house, for no place seems safe from them."

"To be expected at a time like this, I'm afraid," Holmes said commiseratingly. "What of the wedding guests?"

"All gone home, sir, long ago." I saw Holmes's lips tighten in exasperation. "Lady Caroline and the countess have retired to their rooms, and—my lord?"

Behind him the library door had been flung wide, and in the opening stood a man who had been tall and was now much stooped, with a face unhealthily ruddy and a manner short and impatient. His overcoat with its velvet collar, revers, and deep turn-back cuffs was badly worn, the deerskin gloves he was irritably yanking on his hands were so old they were limp, and the soft-felt billycock hat rammed under his arm had seen many years of service. "Mr. Holmes? Dr. Watson?" he inquired abruptly. "That trouble at the charity ball. Last Easter. Mrs. Marshall says you solved it. Quickly. Without fuss."

Holmes bowed. "I was fortunate, Lord Mowbray, for what seemed to be a complex problem turned out to be very simple."

"Do the same here . . . eternally grateful. Whatever they want, Rogers," with a jerk of his head in the butler's direction, "see they have it. Going to my club. Can't stand this row." As if in illustration, a heavy thump came from somewhere across the hall. "That inspector," Lord Mowbray paused to add in exasperation, "is an ass." With which he slammed on his hat and marched out.

A stocky young man in a high-buttoned jacket and striped trousers could be seen standing in a doorway on the far side of the hall. From the flush mounting his cheeks and the narrowing of his deep-set eyes, it was obvious that this was the disparaged inspector.

Rogers gave a tactful little cough. "Mr. Holmes and Dr. Watson, sir, sent for by the countess. Inspector Macready, gentlemen."

"Ah yes," the detective observed distantly, his voice cold and his sturdy chin high. He had, however, the intelligence to realize that, since our presence had the blessing of both the earl and the countess, his feelings were of little importance. With a small shrug he held out his hand. "I don't think we've met, Mr. Holmes, for I'm new to the department, but of course I know of you. And this is Dr. Watson? Well now, if you would like to come along with me, I've no objection to showing you what there is to see. And I don't mind telling you that the case is a corker, a real corker."

The open satisfaction with which he said this jarred on me: this young inspector was all too obviously and confidently looking toward a triumphant conclusion for himself. Holmes said not a word, though I noticed a sardonic smile twitch his lips, and we followed Macready into the massive dining-room, fifty feet wide and stretching from front to back of the house. The high ceiling was an azure blue with intricate flower-moulding swarming out of the corners to form a frame for the star-shaped chandelier, its myriad candles now blackened and neglected, mute evidence of the dismay that had struck the household. Below, running the length of the room, was a huge oak table that could, I am sure, have easily seated fifty, with matching high-backed chairs ornately carved. On the wall facing us was an onyx chimney-piece, flanked by ormolu decorations repeating the flower motif, on the right a huge painting of yet more flowers that appeared rather faded in colour and indefinite in design. On the left wall was the cause of the noise we had heard: an armoire of blackened oak, at least ten feet long and four high, had been shifted a few inches by two panting policemen, who were now peering behind it.

This move in the placing of the furniture was all too evidently only the last of many, for not a single piece, from the damask-covered table to a striped brocade sofa now cutting across one corner, looked to be in its original position. As for the dishes still on the cloth, they could have been set by a blind man, napkins and silverware being scattered about at random and glasses pushed together into a jumble of crystal. Even as we silently surveyed this chaos, a slim young man in the dark-green livery of a footman disappeared out the service door, a large silver dish containing the watery remains of an ice-pudding in his arms and another policeman right at his heels.

Inspector Macready watched this pair vanish with a smile of satisfaction that I was to understand only later. Then, with a flourish of his arm that took in the whole disordered room, he unnecessarily proclaimed, "The scene of the crime!"

"I should say so," Holmes sarcastically agreed.

This didn't as much as scratch the young inspector's self-esteem. "I can give you the case in a nutshell, Mr. Holmes," he began breezily. "Lady Caroline (the bride, you know) wore the Thistle of Scotland in her hair for her wedding this morning. When everyone arrived back from the church, they all came in here—"

"Not in their overcoats and mantles, surely?"

"No, no, of course not, Mr. Holmes. The ladies

went upstairs to the countess's bedroom, and the gentlemen into the library across the hall."

"Which is now bare of overcoats." Holmes's tone was severe.

"Well, you couldn't keep them, Mr. Holmes," the inspector said defensively. "Not people of their standing."

"Couldn't you indeed? Perhaps you have a list of their names?"

"Of course I do. And addresses." The ruffled officer took out a notebook and rapidly flipped over the pages as if to prove his efficiency. "Here you are."

"And the seating plan? You noted that?"

"It's of no importance, Mr. Holmes, as you'll see. Anyway, it was traditional, going according to position in the party and in society, as it were. In the centre of the table, with their backs to the fire, were Lady Caroline and her new husband—"

"I wasn't aware that there was an old husband in existence," Holmes murmured, still busy with his pencil.

This shaft did reach home. The inspector, flushing, hurried on. "Next to the groom was Miss Honoria Powle, the bridesmaid, and next to Lady Caroline her brother, Eustace, the groomsman. Lord Mowbray was on Miss Powle's left, with Lady Louise Eglington next to him."

"Her mother was a favourite at Napoleon's court."

"Really? On the countess's right was Major Charles Epwell—"

"One of the heroes of Balaklava, I believe."

"That so? On the opposite side of the table were the Marchioness of Hartford—"

"The dowager?"

The inspector blinked. "Probably: lady about sixty. She sat across from Major Epwell. Then Mr. Mountford Ashley, Lady James Harley, Lord Withring-ham—"

"A member of the last cabinet," Holmes observed.

"Then Miss Ashley," the inspector continued.

"Thirty years ago she was to have married Lord Braseley. He was killed in a hunting accident on the eve of their wedding. Quite a tragedy."

"Certainly," I agreed, much puzzled by Holmes's persistent offerings of these scraps of biography.

The inspector had given up paying any attention to Holmes's interpolations. "Then Sir James Harley—he's an old school fellow of his lordship's, apparently —Mrs. Marshall and Colonel Edward Brice. That's the lot."

"Thank you. After the ladies had taken off their bonnets and mantles upstairs, and the gentlemen had shed their coats and hats in the library, where did they all go? Not directly here, surely?"

"Well, no, they gathered in the drawing-room for a minute or two, just long enough to sort themselves out, as it were. Then they came down in procession, with the bride and groom leading. Now one and all of these people, Mr. Holmes, people representing some of the best blood in the land, together with Rogers the butler and Seeton the footman, swear that the clip was in Lady Caroline's back hair, and the ame-thyst in the clip, when she sat down at the table. The ornament was particularly conspicuous because her hair was in a sort of bun, with the clip pinned at the top. Not a very fancy hairdo for a wedding, but then," this was said in a lowered voice, "this wasn't a very fancy wedding, for all it was for the daughter of an earl."

"Guests more select than numerous," Holmes suggested gravely.

"Exactly, Mr. Holmes." Apparently the cliché was

new to the inspector. "Now everything during the breakfast went off according to plan, the food and wine served by Rogers and Seeton, and then the toasts. The time came for the groom to say his little piece, and so Mr. Stanley got to his feet, a glass of champagne in his hand. He not unnaturally looked down at his new wife—at his wife," the inspector hastily amended, "went stiff as a board, and cried out, 'The amethyst's gone!' And it *had* gone. Not a doubt about that.

"Well, as you can imagine, that brought on a real uproar. Everybody jumped up except Lady Caroline, and she went as white as the table-cloth and clapped her hands to her head. The clip was still in place in her hair, right enough, but the amethyst was missing. Of course the first thought was that it had somehow fallen out after she sat down, and would be found tangled in her hair, or maybe caught in her dress. So the ladies patted her all over and shook the folds of her skirt and all that. No amethyst. Meanwhile the gentlemen were crawling around the carpet and poking around in the dishes still on the table. No amethyst. Then, in a kind of desperation, Lady Caroline was taken up to her bedroom—"

"By whom?" Holmes asked.

"The countess and Miss Powle. The lady's maid, a girl named Essie Harris, was called in to help too, and I understand Lady Caroline was completely undressed, every garment searched, even her hair brushed out. No amethyst. While all this was going on, the gentlemen extended their search to the hall and the stairs, though they all knew that that was useless. After all, the stone had been in the clip when Lady Caroline sat down at the table, and she'd never moved from there before the stone was found to be missing. At last Lord Mowbray said that the police had got to be called and sent his secretary around to the Herb of Grace, where a couple of the coachmen were waiting until needed, and one of them brought a note to us. Since about noon *we've* been searching. Still no amethyst."

Holmes's eyes roamed once more over the two labouring policemen. The armoire had been returned to its place. Now the undersides of the furniture were being examined. "Quite a pretty little problem."

"You may well say so." The inspector's little eyes were glistening in his enthusiasm. "All the guests stayed at the table right through breakfast. Nobody got up, or touched Lady Caroline's hair, or her gown, or anything like that, and yet the amethyst's gone."

"You have the empty clip, I presume?"

Holmes was looking directly at the inspector's lower-right pocket, which bulged suspiciously. With obvious reluctance Macready drew out a flat red plush box and set it, open, on the table.

Against the scarlet silk lining the four-inch silver stem, with a small elongated leaf on each side, curved gracefully to filigree work that formed the calyx of the thistle. At its back another half-inch of spade-shaped silver topped by three claws had secured the stone. The whole was elegant, of obvious old and meticulous workmanship, yet it now looked bare and bereft without the crowning glory of the purple stone.

Even so Holmes spent several minutes examining the clip with his lens. "The setting has been damaged," he at last observed.

Macready gave a short supercilious laugh. "Of course it has, Mr. Holmes; I didn't need any magnifying glass to show me that. Done to get the amethyst out. You can warrant the stone wasn't loose when the clip arrived at Mowbray House, not when that Manning chap at Gerrard's had had the handling of it."

"Quite so, Inspector. I may keep the clip for the time being?" Macready gave a grudging nod. "Thank you." Holmes scribbled a receipt. "Now what of the servants? Butler and footman busy with serving the breakfast, passing back and forth between the dining-room and the serving alley. Were they both in the room when the stone was found to be missing?" Macready nodded. "How about the other servants?"

"Four women in the kitchen or the alley the whole time, and the lady's maid upstairs from start to finish."

"All been with the family long?"

"The lady's maid is young, but she's the daughter of the old coachman and grew up on Mowbray Park, the family's country place in Kent. The other women are old-timers. The footman, Will Seeton, though, is more recent, about a year."

Before the inspector could add more, what I can only call a blended howl of female voices burst out from below, with the interjection of a series of short male barks that proved quite ineffectual in reducing the crescendo of sound.

Macready pursed his lips in superior disapproval. "I'd better get back to the job on hand, Mr. Holmes. Hawkins is working downstairs, and he doesn't have just the right manner with the women. We've sent for a policewoman for the search, of course, but you can't get servants to see the necessity of it." With an expression that was a mixture of exasperation and satisfaction, the inspector bustled out by the service door.

"If you'll excuse me, sir," a firm little voice came from behind us, "the countess would like to see you."

30

We turned to find an alert-faced wisp of a girl, with lively blue eyes and blond hair wound around her neat head in long braids: obviously this was Essie Harris, the lady's maid. Her dress of Parma-violet serge showed that her small frame yet had room for a becoming female shape, and fitted with a precision that suggested that she was well aware of the fact. Though her speech had the respectful decorum of the well-trained servant, accents and occasional phrases showed her Kentish origin.

"Perhaps you could first take a moment to answer a few questions, Essie," Holmes suggested, "so that we won't have to worry the countess with them. Could we go to the library?"

"I'm yare, sir." She led the way and waited with wide and eager eyes.

"You were upstairs all during the breakfast, I understand," Holmes began.

"Yes, sir. In the countess's bedroom, in case any of the ladies wanted anything."

"And did they?"

"No, sir. Not after they'd all left their bonnets and things when they came from church. Not until the countess and Miss Powle came up with Lady Caroline, her with no more life in her than a chunk, and no wonder."

"Was the search of Lady Caroline's person thorough?"

Essie nodded vigorously. "We started with her wedding dress, and by the time we'd finished we'd taken off every blessed stitch her ladyship had on, and we were right choice in the doing of it, too. I even let her hair down and combed it out ever so careful, but there wasn't as much as a smell of that amethyst."

———

"You, the countess, and Miss Powle were all with Lady Caroline during this search?"

"Oh yes, sir, every second, Lady Caroline being hardly able to do a thing for herself. At last the countess said she'd have to tell them downstairs and went off in tears. Miss Powle offered to stay with Lady Caroline, but my lady just sat there in her dressing gown, staring at herself in the mirror, with her hair all hanging over her shoulders. I tried to do it up again, but she said, 'Go away. Go away, both of you. I want to lie down.' So Miss Powle went downstairs, and I slipped next door into the countess's parlour in case Lady Caroline wanted something, but she's never let out as much as a peep. She's in her room yet, poor lady, lying abed all alone, and this her wedding day." The little maid's own blue eyes had become moist with sympathetic tears.

"Thank you, Essie; that was all very clear. Now if you could help me sketch a plan of each floor of Mowbray House, I won't have to trouble Rogers. On the ground floor, here is the hall, with the library on one side and the dining-room taking up all of the other. That's correct, isn't it? Behind the library are two back parlours? One of them used as a breakfast room, yes. Now up the stairs, and we have the drawing-room on the left, matching the dining-room below? And on the right two more parlours. Now on the second floor no doubt we have the family bedrooms? The countess's chamber at the front, yes, her parlour next to that, then Lady Caroline's room. At the back corner an empty chamber, and then your room? I see. His lordship's room is at the front, on the opposite side of the hall; next to him his secretary, next to him Mr. Eustace, and another empty room. And the third floor isn't used now? Quite. Thank you, Essie."

"Hadn't we better go up to the countess, sir?"

"We had, certainly, though I wonder if we could first see Lady Caroline's wedding gown."

"If you don't mind waiting in the hall, sir, I'll see if I can slip in and get it for you."

This she did, after leading us up two sets of graceful stairs of painted balustrades and moulded plasterwork. Lady Caroline, Essie reported sadly, was now sitting by the window, staring out, and had paid "not a farthing" of attention to Essie, not even when she took up the wedding gown, for all it was, as Essie said, "brave enough for a Pharisee queen."

The dress had obviously been chosen to complement the lost amethyst, being of lavender and silver brocade. It had long sleeves gathered to narrow cuffs, a fitted cuirass bodice with a high stand collar, and a skirt gathered to wide pleats at the back. The left shoulder was damp, which Essie said was from her sponging to remove the stain of the champagne the bridegroom had spilled when he had discovered that the amethyst had gone. Holmes returned the gown to Essie, she took it back to Lady Caroline's bedroom, still arousing no interest from the poor bride, and we were then led to the countess's parlour.

This was the only room I ever saw at Mowbray House that held more of present comfort than dead grandeur. Comparatively small, it was graced by a white-and-gold Adam fireplace with some really fine string-moulding. Though a rather unexpected round mirror with a rococo frame took the place of an overmantel, at least the shadowed silver of the glass was kind to the threadbare cretonne covers and faded velvet of the curtains, and if the Turkey carpet was well worn, it still retained much of its brave maroon colour.

The countess suited the room, a tall woman with an echo of beauty still in her plentiful light-brown hair and soft pale skin. I should think her manner had always been vague, and was now near frantic. So upset was she that as soon as the door was opened, she rushed toward us, dropping a frame of tapestry work and scattering skeins of silk. "Oh, Mr. Holmes," she cried, the grey lace of her princess-style gown billowing around her, "whatever are we to do?"

"You have already done much, Countess," he replied with kind firmness while I gathered up the frame and the silks. "Lord Mowbray sent for the police—"

"Oh yes, he had to. Yes, at once. At least very soon. But—"

"And *you* sent for *me,*" Holmes finished magnificently and made a superb bow.

I know it sounds absurd, but such was Holmes's manner at such moments that I, as a doctor, could only think what a bedside manner he would have had! Certainly the countess quietened at once, and a hint of a smile even touched her white lips. "Why, yes, Mr. Holmes, it *was* I who sent for you. Because of Agnes—Mrs. Marshall, you know. She kept saying that you had been so clever about Cynthia's brooch. Lady Arnley, you remember, and that Blue-school charity ball where she lost it. But," the countess had taken out a fragment of handkerchief and was twisting it helplessly between her hands, "Cynthia's brooch was only stolen. Caroline's amethyst . . . it's *vanished.*"

"You don't think the amethyst too has been stolen?"

"How could it have been, Mr. Holmes?" The

countess made a sudden dash for the bell and gave it a distracted pull. "Let us have tea. I always think tea helps, don't you? The amethyst *couldn't* have been stolen, Mr. Holmes, for we were all there, sitting around the table. No one went near Caroline, except of course Will and Rogers—"

"You rang, my lady?" Rogers had quietly opened the door and must have heard the countess's last words. Was the increased pallor of his face the result?

"Tea," the countess ordered, with an agitated flap of her hand. "Tea, Rogers. Here, at once." As Rogers departed, I had the feeling that the countess's orders were always given in this way, and that they were accordingly discounted by the servants before they were obeyed. Certainly in this case the tea-tray was long in coming.

We were by now seated around a little inlaid table, and Holmes with his usual quiet skill proceeded to lead the countess through a full account of the events. "No doubt Lady Caroline was excited when she heard of her inheritance?" he began.

"Oh, certainly, Mr. Holmes. What girl wouldn't be? And so unexpected, you know. Even I hadn't seen Lady Picton since Caroline's christening, and Caroline didn't know her at all. But of course poor Helen really had no one else to leave the amethyst clip to, her son and grandson both drowning in that terrible accident. Such a treacherous coast off the Forth, isn't it? They should never have been permitted to go out, not that I expect they would have listened. Men don't, do they? And now the amethyst has gone too. . . . Oh dear, it's all so sad!" Here two tears trickled down the countess's soft face, and were dabbed away with the crumpled handkerchief.

———

"Lord Mowbray must be facing a special problem," Holmes said carefully, "as I understand that the amethyst clip has already been sold."

The countess nodded wearily. "Such a pity, isn't it? But there was no choice, Mr. Holmes. Our family is really quite poor now, you know, and Caroline had nothing until this inheritance. It seemed a true godsend, and now—"

"Have you and Lord Mowbray known Mr. Adolphus Stanley long?"

Open astonishment filled the countess's pale face. "Oh, I don't know him at all, Mr. Holmes. Lord Mowbray had heard of him, of course, the way men do, for I understand that Mr. Stanley is quite a familiar figure in the City, and I think Eustace had met him somewhere. At a club probably, though Eustace doesn't belong to any now, but these young men *do* gather together, don't they? And of course once the preliminary negotiations proved satisfactory"—this was an obvious quotation from the family lawyer—"Mr. Stanley dined here so that he and Caroline could meet."

"And that too was . . . satisfactory?"

"Oh yes," the countess replied austerely. "Caroline is a dear good girl," she added, "and quite understood the situation."

"Let me see if I have the dates correct. When did Lady Caroline hear of her inheritance?"

"When Lord Mowbray's lawyer received a letter from Lady Picton's legal man, near the end of September."

"I see. When did Mr. Stanley approach Lord Mowbray?"

"Very soon. Within a few days, I think."

"The family was in London at that time?"

The countess shook her head. "We used to come

36

up for the season, for Caroline's sake, but Lord Mowbray didn't feel we could afford to do so this year. Of course once we heard from the lawyer about Mr. Stanley's letter, we came at once."

"No doubt after Mr. Stanley and Lady Caroline met, he has been a frequent visitor here? Naturally. Now, countess, could you explain how the Thistle of Scotland was handled today? According to the papers, it was to be brought here this morning by Mr. Manning of Gerrard's."

At this something like a child's delight crept over the countess's woebegone face. "That was what the papers *said*," she agreed, "but that was all a story, Mr. Holmes. To deceive the thieves, you see. Mr. Manning did come this morning, with two great big policemen, but really he had brought the clip about seven o'clock last night. A policeman came then too, but in ordinary clothes so no one who saw them would guess that they weren't regular visitors."

"Why was the clip brought here so long before the wedding?"

"Because Caroline wanted to wear it for a little dinner party we were giving for her. Just the family and Miss Powle and Mrs. Marshall. And Mr. Stanley, of course."

"Did he have any objections to Lady Caroline's wearing the clip for the dinner? Or for the wedding?"

"None at all, though having it here overnight did make us all a bit anxious."

"Then why not have returned it to Gerrard's until this morning?"

"Because that would have meant having Mr. Manning come here again quite late last evening, and if any gang—of thieves, you know—had been watching, it would have been quite obvious that he wouldn't be making a social call at that time of night.

So we decided that once the clip had arrived here, it would be safer for it to stay.

"Then when the amethyst disappeared right in our own dining-room," the countess's eyes again filled with tears, "and everything was so... so terrible, no one thought to send word to Mr. Manning. So he came this afternoon as had been arranged, to take the clip back to Gerrard's. When I explained what had happened, Mr. Manning turned so white that I thought he'd faint. He kept saying that he'd stake his life that the amethyst had been perfectly tight in its setting when the clip had left his hands, and didn't seem to hear me when I assured him that no one doubted that. He even wanted to see Caroline, to express his sympathy, though of course she had gone to her room, and I didn't disturb her. Oh dear, Mr. Holmes—"

"Whose clever idea was it," Holmes interrupted smoothly, "to let the newspapers spread the word that the clip wouldn't be brought until this morning?"

"Lord Mowbray's," his wife said loyally. "Or it might have been Mr. Torbram's, his secretary's; he's a very quick young man. Or did Eustace... No, I'm sure it couldn't have been Eustace who thought of it. However, one of them did."

"So Mr. Manning brought the clip last evening and gave it to Lady Caroline?"

"To Lord Mowbray, really, in the drawing-room, where we all were. Lord Mowbray opened the case and handed it to Caroline; she passed it to me, and I gave it to Miss Powle, and she to... Eustace, I think. After we had all admired the clip, Miss Powle took it out and fastened it in Caroline's hair, then we all went down to dinner. And nothing happened to the amethyst *then*," the countess concluded for-lornly.

"And after dinner?" Holmes pressed.

"Why," the countess paused helplessly, "the guests left. Caroline took the clip out of her hair and put it into her jewel box—"

"Not into the plush case?"

"Oh no, Mr. Holmes, that didn't have a lock. Caroline had had Essie bring one of her own boxes down. She put the clip in, locked the box, and gave it, with the key still in the lock, to Lord Mowbray. And then she and I—oh, and Eustace—went up to bed."

"So Lord Mowbray kept the clip, in the jewel box, all night?"

The countess shook her head. "Mr. Torbram and that guard man watched over it somewhere upstairs."

Certainly extracting information from the poor countess was like pulling molars. But Holmes persisted with never a sign of impatience. "What guard man, my lady?"

"Someone that Lord Mowbray had hired. A retired policeman, I think he was. He'd been waiting in servants' hall, and after the guests had gone Rogers showed him up. I don't know anything more about it, Mr. Holmes, for it was all kept secret. For safety, you see. And whatever the plan was," the countess added, with a sudden burst of energy, "it worked, for nothing happened to the clip through the night. This morning Miss Powle came, and when we were all in the drawing-room ready to leave for church, Rogers sent Will upstairs—"

"So Rogers knew where the clip was being kept?"

The countess looked surprised. "Why . . . why, yes,

39

I suppose he did; Rogers knows everything. And Mr. Torbram came down with this guard man behind him, and gave the jewel box to Lord Mowbray. He took the key out of his pocket and undid the box, Miss Powle fastened the clip in Caroline's hair, and then we all left for the church."

"All," Holmes repeated. "Lady Caroline, Miss Powle, Mr. Eustace, you and Lord Mowbray. Anyone else, Countess?"

"Not from here, Mr. Holmes. Oh, Will, to see to the vehicles and rugs and such forth. Mr. Stanley and the other guests had gone directly to the church, of course."

"Of course. Why, by the way, was the wedding at St. George's? It isn't your parish church, is it?"

The countess shook her head. "It was Caroline's choice. I really don't know why."

"I see. Now as to the breakfast." Holmes took the countess through all the details, but no useful information emerged: as far as the countess recalled, all had gone in the usual way of such social events until the shocking conclusion. She was certainly emphatic that no one had moved from the table until then.

Holmes then asked if he could examine the jewel box and also see Lady Caroline, apologizing for the necessity of both and promising not to keep the poor bride long.

"I'll go to her myself," the countess said, "for with the staff so upset and those policemen everywhere I really don't know. . ." She sailed out with a purposeful rustle of skirts.

"You have quite revived that poor lady's spirits," I commented.

"Not with lasting effect, I fear."

———

"You have as yet no idea what has happened to the amethyst?"

Holmes shook his head. "I wish most heartily that we could have arrived before the police, for it is impossible to make anything now out of the chaos in the dining-room. As for the clip itself," he took the plush case from his pocket and handed it and his lens to me, "what do you make of the damage it has sustained?"

Even without the glass it was obvious that the calyx that had held the amethyst was no longer perfectly smooth and that the three tiny claws at the top were bent. But looking closely I could see that the claws had been roughly pushed down, not up, as I had expected, and that the filigree work too had been somewhat squashed, not lifted. Puzzled, I used the lens and only saw more clearly what I had already noted.

"Holmes," I said, staring at him in astonishment, "it's as if the setting has been *tightened,* not loosened!"

"I agree. The claws and the calyx have been forced toward the stone, not away from it."

"But that makes no sense!" I exclaimed. "To begin with, altered in this way, the setting couldn't hold the amethyst. And what thief would tighten the setting in order to remove the stone?"

The parlour door opened, and a tall and slender young woman stood facing us, a small carved box in her hand.

———

Chapter III

Your eye shall light upon some toy
—Shakespeare, *Twelfth Night,*
act 3, sc. 3, line 44

"**M**r. Holmes?"

Lady Caroline's voice was low and distant, matching the still dignity of her posture. She was as tall as the countess, slender, and, with her deep-blue dress touched with white lace at the throat and wrists, she stood framed in the dark doorway like the regal portrait of some bygone queen.

Then she slowly stepped into the room, into the last rays of the sun that had found their way over the chimney-pots of London. At once the pallor of her oval face was cruelly clear, the seeming rich silk of her dress reduced to poplin, the lace trim revealed as much darned, and the slim white hands that clasped the rosewood box pathetically trembling.

"This is very good of you, Lady Caroline." Holmes set a chair for her near the small fire, and, taking the jewel box from her, spent a moment examining it. "I will try to be as brief as I can."

Lady Caroline's bravely held head, with its thick dark hair bundled loosely in a net, inclined regally, but then stayed bent. Her left hand remained clenched in her lap, her right had disappeared into a pocket that hung from her waist, and there could be seen clutching something tightly.

"Did you take any part in the arrangements for the guarding of the hair clip last night?" Holmes began.

"No."

"Then let us move to the events of this morning. Have you any idea how the stone came to disappear?"

An emphatic shake of the still-bowed head.

"Did anything out of the ordinary, no matter how slight, occur during the breakfast?"

"I noticed nothing." Very low.

"Did anyone, for any reason, rise from the table before the toasts began?"

"I don't think so." A mere murmur.

"When Mr. Stanley cried out that the amethyst had gone, what did you do?"

"I don't remember." Barely audible.

"I realize that this is all very hard for you, Lady Caroline," Holmes said gently.

At this she abruptly rose and, without a glance in our direction, moved quickly toward the door. There she paused. "It's the waiting," she said, with sudden vehemence and without turning. "Not knowing what he . . ." She broke off and, jerking her right hand from her pocket, reached for the doorknob. With the sudden movement something small and roundish fell to the floor.

Two rolling dots of eyes seemed to blink up at me. I was so startled that I simply stood fixed, staring stupidly down at whatever it was that was apparently

43

bounding toward me. Holmes, though, had at once darted forward, and now, scooping up the little object, held it out to Lady Caroline. And what an incongruous thing it was! Grinning up from Holmes's outstretched palm was one of those gutta-percha toy heads that were so popular with mischievous young boys a few years ago, its rubbery features twisted into a pop-eyed scowl.

Lady Caroline, flushing angrily, snatched up the plaything, hastily stuffed it back into her pocket, and reached again for the closed door. It opened without her touch to reveal Rogers with the tea-tray, behind him the indistinct shape of a young man.

"I say, old girl," this dithering apparition urged in a reedy tenor, "have a cup of tea or a biscuit or something. Do, now."

To this appeal Lady Caroline paid not the slightest attention. Brushing rapidly by, she disappeared into the deep dusk of the hall.

Rogers brought in the tray, with the young man trailing into the parlour after him. "This is Mr. Holmes and Dr. Watson, sir," the butler explained deferentially, setting the tray on the low table before us. "Mr. Eustace Mowbray, gentlemen. Shall I pour out, sir?"

"Let me have a go," the young man offered dolefully. "You're probably wanted downstairs—there's an awful row goin' on, I can tell you—and at least I can pretend I'm doin' something useful here."

Eustace Mowbray was no taller than his sister and just as slender, but whereas Lady Caroline was dark, Eustace was very fair, the straight hair slicked to his head so light that it looked bleached. His eyes were a watery blue, the little moustache he affected served only to call attention to his decidedly rabbity teeth, and his single-breasted morning coat, high-shouldered and high-waisted, topped by a high wing collar and a splendidly folded cravat, was so elegant that he looked more like a manikin than a living figure. Yet his manner was so self-deprecating that one automatically rather liked him, while at the same time finding it impossible to take him seriously. I could imagine that he had heard an exasperated chorus of "Oh, *Eustace!*" all his life.

He had seated himself at the little table and now proceeded to pour out the tea, adding cream and sugar with a neat quickness that made me notice the nervous flexibility of his thin hands. "The governor," he observed plaintively, dexterously handling the plate of ratafia biscuits, "told me to stay around in case I was wanted. But what's the good of that? Nobody'll want *me.*" His pale blinking eyes and weedily drooping figure made that seem all too likely.

"You can certainly be of use to us, Mr. Mowbray," Holmes assured him, "if you don't mind answering a few questions."

"Mind?" Eustace sat up eagerly. "My dear chap, be delighted. Mrs. Marshall's given you such a buildup, don't you know," he added earnestly. "'Send for Mr. Holmes of Baker Street,' she kept telling the mater. 'The police are all very well, my dear, but you send for Mr. Holmes.' And I must say that that inspector feller has made an almighty hash of things downstairs. The women in hysterics, Will invisible, Rogers run off his feet. No luncheon, ring a bell, and nobody comes. What's the use of it all? I mean, the servants haven't taken the bally amethyst."

"Who has?" Holmes asked bluntly.

———

"Don't ask *me*, Mr. Holmes. *I* don't have any ideas." Indeed, Eustace looked quite terrified at the thought.

"Then perhaps you will give me your opinion of Lady Caroline's marriage to Mr. Stanley."

"Best thing that could have happened," Eustace replied promptly. "No secret about that, don't you know. The governor'd be free of all the milliner's bills and such forth, and the mater wouldn't have to bother any more about doin' the season. Perfectly ridiculous the things girls have to do to get married."

"You aren't married yourself, Mr. Mowbray?" My question was nearly inadvertent and certainly uncalled for, but he answered without hesitation.

"Couldn't possibly, Dr. Watson. No money, you know, and the estate entailed and in a beastly mess."

"Would Lady Caroline's marriage have helped *you* at all?" Holmes asked.

"Not exactly helped," the young man said cautiously, "though it can't hurt a feller to have a brother-in-law on 'Change, don't you know. And I might've been able to stay with Cal and Stanley now and then, what with the governor intendin' to let this place year-round once Cal was off his hands. Now I suppose it's all off."

"You don't mean the marriage?" I asked in amazement.

"No stone, no five thousand pounds. No five thousand pounds, no marriage," Eustace replied succinctly, "and the blasted stone's gone. Ain't no doubt about that, is there?"

"But the wedding was this morning," I protested, "so the marriage has already been made."

"Marriages can be unmade," Eustace returned, "if the couple don't set up housekeepin' together.

And Stanley took himself off soon's he'd had a word with the police, don't you know. Said he couldn't do anything more to help, so would make himself scarce."

"Is Lady Caroline aware of all this?" I demanded, quite appalled by the cold practicality of the whole thing, and haunted too by the memory of that pale figure retreating from even Holmes's gentle questioning, having to wait until "he" should decide her fate.

"Cal ain't a fool, Doctor," her brother replied laconically. "All-round it's a poor look-out for the old girl, unless you chaps can come up with something."

"We will at least do our best," Holmes assured him. "How well do you know Mr. Stanley?"

"I?" Eustace looked quite startled. "Oh, I don't *know* the feller at all. Met him around the clubs and all that. Nothing more."

"What clubs does Mr. Stanley belong to?"

"'Pon my word, I don't know. Seen him at White's and dinin' once or twice with Mellenberg and that crowd. Something to do with some property, or so they say. That's about all. He don't play, at least I've never seen him take a hand."

"Yet you were his groomsman?"

Eustace hesitated, his acquired sense of decorum in obvious conflict with his innate loquacity. The latter won. "The governor'd insisted that the number of guests be kept deuced small. To save the shekels, you see. The mater had to ask Stanley if he'd keep his list of invites to the minimum, and he said the mater could have it all, and if I'd trot along beside him, that was fine with him. Behaved like the perfect gent about it all, don't you know. The mater was ever so bucked."

"Mr. Stanley must have wanted the marriage very badly," Holmes observed, to my considerable discomfiture.

"He wanted the five thousand pounds, that's right enough, and wanted it soon. There ain't so many places a feller can pick that kind of money up, not without payin' for the privilege, and that ain't Stanley's style. Besides, though it ain't quite the thing to say, marryin' an earl's daughter can be useful to a chappie like that, don't you know."

"Are you certain that the amethyst was in Lady Caroline's hair when she entered the dining-room this morning?"

"Couldn't be more positive, Mr. Holmes. I took Miss Powle in, she bein' the bridesmaid, so we were on Caroline's heels, and that amethyst was glitterin' like a deuced drop of pink bubbly all the time. Oh, it was there then, no doubt about that."

"When Mr. Stanley rose to give the toast and then cried out that the stone had gone, what did Lady Caroline do?"

"Went white as the table-cloth, red, and back to white again. Clapped her hands to her mouth."

"To her mouth, not her hair?"

"First to her mouth, like this." And the young man jerked his open palms up to his lower face and then, with another convulsive movement that was very convincing mimicry, to the back of his head. "The way girls do when they're startled, don't you know."

"And Mr. Stanley?"

"Just stood there stammerin' and flappin' his napkin at Cal. He'd spilled champagne over her, you see. Terrible waste of good stuff; the governor hadn't spared any expense there, I'll say that for him."

"How large *is* the amethyst? Compared to this emerald, for instance?" Holmes had risen to lean against the mantel, and, having taken his tie-pin from his pocket, turned the stone so that it caught the firelight.

Eustace cocked his head for a moment of consideration. "Four times that size, I'd say."

"Really?" I exclaimed, for Holmes's emerald is really very handsome.

"Every bit of it," Eustace affirmed. "No mistake, Dr. Watson, that Thistle stone is a whopper. That's what seems so funny, don't you know, about its disappearin' like that. I mean, you'd think it'd show up wherever it had fallen. But we looked everywhere, really did. I even poked the ice-puddin' to pieces. Swan, with glass eyes. Eyes both there, not the right colour, and not a fraction of the size of the amethyst anyway. *I* don't know, Mr. Holmes. I mean, it's a demned mystery, don't you know."

A tap came on the door, and a sombrely dressed young man looked in. "Oh, excuse me, Mr. Mowbray."

"Here's the feller you want!" Eustace exclaimed, jumping to his feet. "Wade Torbram, the governor's secretary and a frightfully bright chap. He'll help you if anyone can. Nothin' else I can do, is there? No, 'course not." With a relieved smile and a nod, Eustace took his elegant self off.

Lord Mowbray's secretary was tall and a little portly for his thirty-odd years, with a hair-line well receding and steady brown eyes behind steel-rimmed spectacles. "The countess asked me to see if you gentlemen would stay for dinner. She also told me I must warn you that it is very uncertain as to what and when dinner will be, for the police are still downstairs and servants' hall is an emotional quagmire."

"We won't trespass further on the countess's kindness," Holmes replied. "Perhaps you would just explain the plan adopted to guard the Thistle of Scotland during the night."

"Quite simple, Mr. Holmes. We led the newspapers to believe that it would be brought from Gerrard's this morning; in reality it was brought last evening."

"For Lady Caroline to wear for a dinner party here, I understand."

Torbram nodded. "We were a little worried that someone in the underworld might not be fooled by the newspaper accounts, be watching the house, see Mr. Manning call last evening with a sturdy companion who could only be a police escort, guess the reason, and proceed to make an attempt on the house during the night. So foiling any such effort was our chief concern."

"When you say 'our concern,' Mr. Torbram, you are referring to Lord Mowbray and yourself?"

"The countess and Mr. Mowbray had some suggestions," the secretary answered tactfully. "Our problem was made more acute by there no longer being a safe here."

"What is done with the household valuables?"

"There is virtually nothing now that qualifies as such. We bring a little plate with us from Mowbray Park when we come up to London, and that of course is kept in the butler's pantry."

"What of the countess's and Lady Caroline's jewels?"

"I'm afraid they have none that would interest a professional thief, Mr. Holmes; a few keepsakes, that is all." Torbram rose and took a candlestick from the mantel. "If you'd care to come upstairs, I'll show you what we arranged."

We went up a flight of uncarpeted stairs at the back

of the house, emerging in a long bare corridor that was divided by a central block. Two doors led into this, one on each side, half a dozen more lined each branch of the hall, and on the short blank wall, next to one of the doors, were set a small table and two chairs.

"This floor contains the maids' quarters," Torbram explained, "not needed now. The downstairs staff live off the kitchen and Essie Harris has a room at the back of the floor below this."

"Your own chambers are also on that floor, Mr. Torbram?"

He nodded. "Next to his lordship. Now all these rooms along here"—he waved to the two sides of the corridor—"naturally have windows, which are fairly close to the roof. What we wanted was somewhere that had no outside access at all. This is what we selected."

He opened the first door to that centre island, revealing a small bathroom. An old galvanized tub stood in one corner, a closed commode chair in another, with between a wash-stand with a chipped enamel basin and jug.

"As you'll see," Torbram pointed out proudly, "there is no window, so a forced entry from without was impossible."

"There must be an outside opening of some kind, surely," Holmes suggested, gazing around as he slowly stepped into the room. "Feel the draught." As he spoke he swiftly stooped to pick up something from the dark-painted floor.

"Nothing important there, surely, Mr. Holmes?" Torbram asked, peering down.

"Certainly not the missing amethyst. The room has been mopped out recently, I see."

"Rogers insisted on that, once he knew we were to

---

use this floor. I believe the bathroom and corridor were washed over a couple of days ago."

"If I could trouble you for the candle... Thank you." Holmes held the guttering light up to reveal a screen-covered circular opening in the slanted ceiling above the commode. "Ah, here is the source of the draught."

"A vent to the roof," Torbram explained, "and barely six inches across. Far too small to have been of any danger."

"An elbow pipe?" Holmes had removed the screen, which was loose, and inserted his hand. "Yes, and no wonder there's a draught: even the little rain water that has dripped down is frozen solid."

"It *is* cold up here," Torbram agreed. "Completely unheated, you see."

"So last evening, after the guests had all departed, the servants retired—"

"Except for Rogers. He attended his lordship to his room."

"Quite. Before then you had received the Thistle of Scotland, locked into a rosewood jewel box, from Lord Mowbray?"

"I had, in the drawing-room. Then Griffiths and I—"

"Griffiths?"

"A retired officer, recommended by the police and hired by Lord Mowbray as an extra precaution for the night. We brought the jewel box up here, and I set it on the back of the commode stand. Then we sat at this table," leading the way back into the hall, "Griffiths facing the back and I the front, for the rest of the night. And a cold time we had of it too, I assure you."

This I could well believe, for already my feet were tingling and the end of my nose felt numb.

———

"In the morning, about nine-thirty," Torbram continued, "Will, the footman, came up to tell us the family was ready to leave for the church. I collected the jewel box, we all went down, and I delivered it to Lord Mowbray in the drawing-room. Then Griffiths and I retired, he to servants' hall for his breakfast and I to my room for the same purpose. The dining-room was already set for the wedding meal, of course. And very ready for our bacon and eggs Griffiths and I were."

"During the journey to and from the church, and in the church itself," Holmes asked, "had any special safety precautions been taken?"

"Oh yes, Mr. Holmes. Two police officers came with the party."

"In uniform?"

Torbram nodded. "Since their presence was meant as a deterrent, it was thought best for them to be conspicuous; they arrived, all blue coats and brass buttons, with the hired coach. The countess wasn't too pleased with the decorum of the arrangement, but Lord Mowbray was quite adamant."

"The police did not remain on the premises once the family returned here from church?"

"No, they didn't. As there were quite enough men present, including two retired army officers, not to mention a couple of coachmen waiting nearby at the Herb of Grace, the continued presence of the police was felt to be quite unnecessary. I think that it was, for there was no disturbance of any kind, none, until the stone was found to be missing, and then the police were soon sent for. Whether they'll be able to recover the amethyst... Well, we must hope. Now if you've finished up here, Mr. Holmes—"

"These other chambers," Holmes said, walking

across the hall. "This second one in the centre section, for instance, back to back with the bathroom?"

"That is just a lumber room." Torbram opened the door to reveal an empty space the same size and shape as the bathroom, though without the cold draught from the roof vent. "For the servants' boxes and such forth. 'The rest,' crossing the hall and flinging wide the first of the doors, 'are, as I said, the sleeping quarters for the maids in the days when Mowbray House had a large staff.'"

None of these chambers had more furnishings than old iron beds, with an occasional deal chest of drawers, battered wardrobe, or rickety chair, and I could see nothing of interest in any. Yet while Torbram stood by in courteous patience and I in shivering bemusement, Holmes went from side to side of the corridor, making a quick examination of each room.

"The house is empty most of the year?" I asked Torbram.

He shook his head. "It's rented to some political gentlemen when the family is not in residence; we are just across the river from the Houses of Parliament, you see. Why, whatever have you found now, Mr. Holmes?"

We had reached the small room closest to the stairs. In the bottom drawer of a battered highboy was a pile of roughly folded men's clothing: a dingy tweed cap, a dark-brown jacket of harsh tweed, two well-worn black boots, and a pair of check trousers whose hideous saffron pattern seemed vaguely familiar.

"Well!" Torbram exclaimed with a laugh. "I can't say I blame whatever lad left that outfit behind. I don't think you'll find anything helpful there," for

Holmes had his lens out and was taking a close look at the cloth cap.

"The lining has been replaced at some time in the past," Holmes observed, "by someone clever with the needle. As for the jacket, nothing in the pockets." He raised the garment to his nose. "Been cleaned with Benzedrine, and carefully darned at the elbows. One of the buttons doesn't match, but they're all sturdily sewn on. Buttonholes gone over too. The trousers... Yes, also cleaned and patched. As for the boots, soled and later half-soled as well; not worth mending again, I fancy. How long is it since these rooms were used for staff, Mr. Torbram?"

"I hardly know. Not regularly since I've been with Lord Mowbray, and that's nearly five years."

"Used occasionally?"

"Very seldom. Two or three years ago when Mr. Mowbray brought a friend home for a few days, and the young gentleman had his valet with him, he was put up here somewhere, I remember. I don't think any of the rooms has been occupied since."

"The parliamentary renters don't use this floor?"

"They don't require the space. In fact, they don't use even all the rooms downstairs."

"Has Inspector Macready been to this floor?"

"He has, though he took only a cursory look at the bathroom and corridor."

I noticed Holmes's small smile of satisfaction as he returned the old garments to the drawer, though I couldn't guess its cause. We were soon back in the downstairs hall, and, though that was far from warm, there being no fire in the hearth, it seemed so after the bone-gripping chill of that third floor.

———

"Sure you gentlemen won't dine?" Torbram hospitably urged.

"Thank you, no," Holmes replied. "Could you give me the address of that retired policeman who was on guard with you last night?"

"Certainly, if you'll wait a moment." Torbram led us back into the library, and, opening a drawer of the desk, took out a notebook. "Three or four former officers were recommended by the police, Griffiths one of them. Here we are: Samuel Griffiths, 46 Garden Row. Off Tottenham Court Road."

"Thank you." Holmes took the notebook and scribbled quickly in his own. "You chose Griffiths yourself, Mr. Torbram?"

"Lord Mowbray did. I know our safekeeping schemes sound a little melodramatic, Mr. Holmes," the secretary added, "but at least you'll have to admit that they were successful. Nothing happened to the Thistle of Scotland during the night, of that we can be sure."

"What do you think happened this morning?"

The big man raised his hands helplessly. "How can I say? I didn't even know of the amethyst's disappearance until I heard the commotion, came down, and almost at once was sent by Lord Mowbray to find one of the waiting coachmen to go for the police. My first feeling, I must say, was deep thankfulness that nothing untoward had happened while Griffiths and I were on guard during the night." Torbram paused as he prepared to open the front door for us. "You've no idea how much this marriage means to the whole family, Mr. Holmes."

"Mr. Mowbray said, 'No amethyst, no five thousand pounds. No five thousand pounds, no marriage,'" Holmes observed.

"A harsh comment, but I'm afraid an accurate one.

Did you notice that old mirror above the hearth in the countess's parlour? It replaces a Gibbons over-mantel, one of the last such good pieces in the private rooms of Mowbray House. Sold to pay for the wedding and the cost of the family's extended stay in town."

"All the pictures are copies, of course." Holmes was looking up at a Gainsborough-like portrait of an elderly man in garter robes, which hung over the hearth.

"And not even good copies," Torbram agreed rue-fully. "This one, of the third earl, is not much short of an atrocity. The original had the earl resting his hand on a terrestrial globe, showing in brilliant detail what was then known of the new world. The copyist wouldn't even attempt to reproduce that; hence the ridiculous blob of an urn you see. Did you notice the painting of a vase of flowers in the dining-room? Yes, it's rather unavoidable, isn't it? I've seen better pictures done in worsted. But what can you expect when five pounds have to do the work of a hundred?"

"The library appears to have been much depleted also."

"That has been going on for decades. Even when I first came there was very little left of any interest to bibliophiles. I have catalogued what there is and am trying to find buyers." The secretary sighed. "The stalls of Wyeth or Holywell streets will be our only customers, I fear."

He opened the front door, and we stepped outside. "There is no officer here now." Holmes turned from the top step. "The police haven't left?"

"Oh no." Torbram gave a tired smile. "Inspector Macready is still hard at work in servants' hall, and a man is going to stay on duty outside all night. It's

guarding the empty barn, I'm afraid, but still..."
With a nod, he shut the door, and we were left to the
dark and bitter cold of the night.

"Holmes," I said as we started down the steps,
"those men's clothes in that highboy drawer upstairs. Can they be what that young fellow was wearing whom we saw with Fitzgerald a few weeks ago?"

"I think they must be. At least I should hate to
think there are two pairs of such trousers in existence."

"But what has a man like Fitzgerald to do with
Mowbray House?"

"That is something we will have to find out."

"That footman," I began. "From the glimpse I had
of him, I would say he was slight of build and not too
tall, rather like that young chap in the trousers. You
don't think he and Fitzgerald..." I could go no farther, and Holmes made no answer.

He was staring up at a rather straggling plane tree
that was growing close to the side of Mowbray
House. "Those top branches," he said abruptly. He
had taken out his pocket lantern and was now light-
ing it. "They appear to be very close to that second-
floor window." Without more ado he left the walk,
headed to the tree, sprang into the lower branches,
and disappeared from my sight.

From what I could judge by the movement of the
small light, Holmes paused here and there as he
climbed, and then spent some moments near that
second-floor window. I know I was striding up and
down, stamping my feet on the iron-hard ground and
beating my arms in a futile effort to keep warm, by
the time he jumped down to my side.

"Come, Watson," he extinguished his lantern and
led a brisk pace out the gate, "we'll look for a cab. In

fact, perhaps we had better have two, for no doubt you'll wish to return home."

"I'll send Mary a note and stay on the hunt."

"Splendid. I must see the bridegroom and the bridesmaid, also that guard chap, and all the wedding guests. Far too much for one evening, I'm afraid. Let us at least start with Adolphus Stanley. Good: here's a cab." He gave the driver an address off Rathbone Place, adding that he should keep an eye open as we neared Whitehall for a special messenger. "Do you know," Holmes observed as we started off, "someone else has climbed that tree recently."

"Some neighborhood lad on a prank," I suggested, pulling my scarf up.

"Perhaps. But the activity has occurred more than once, the last time quite recently, and on each occasion the climber has begun and ended by that second-floor window, which opens on the upper hall."

"The family bedrooms are on that floor," I remembered.

"As well as those of Wade Torbram and Essie Harris."

We crossed the handsome arches of Westminster Bridge without further conversation, moving in a cloud of steam from the horse's breath and our own, and turned right on Whitehall. As Holmes had anticipated, we had travelled only a short distance before our driver pulled up and, with a stertorous bellow of "Boy!" produced an aged chap with more buttons than hairs, who took my note for Mary.

As we started off again, Holmes made one of his interjected comments. "Have you been by Buckingham Palace lately, Doctor?"

"Yes," I said, wondering what the queen's official

London residence had to do with Lady Caroline's lost amethyst.

"The rebuilding of the front is going on at a good pace."

"Yes," I again agreed.

"Did you know that what is being added is nothing more than a façade? To make a more attractive appearance. That is what I feel at present about the case: there is a façade that has been added to the essentials. What and by whom I do not yet know, but it is there, Watson, it is there."

We wheeled briskly down Charing Cross Road, so nearly deserted on this cold Sunday night that we seemed to be the only moving things on the street. After a short journey by the handsome buildings of New Oxford Street, we turned first right on Rathbone Place, then quickly right again, and stopped.

"We'd better keep the cab," Holmes said, opening the apron.

I looked out in disbelief. "This is where Adolphus Stanley lives?"

"It is certainly the address the inspector gave me. Not exactly Albany, is it?"

It certainly wasn't. The house at which we had pulled up was in the middle of a two-storey terrace of shabby brick, with a garden represented by half a dozen feet of frozen grass around a hideous monkey-puzzle tree and fenced by rusting iron spikes. The door, an unadorned panel with neither light in it nor transom over it, was opened by an elderly manservant in a very well-worn black coat and grey trousers.

After taking up Holmes's card, he quickly showed us to a room neither large nor even well-lit. The walls were of dark-green paint, the floor bare except for a small square of drugget in the centre, and the only prominent item of furniture was a large walnut desk, covered with neat packets of papers. Behind this stood Adolphus Stanley.

He was older than I had expected, being perhaps in his early forties, above average height, very lean, with grey plentifully sprinkling his black hair and severely clipped moustache. He was dressed in a high-collared coat, with minimal display of shirt and tie; he held gold-rimmed spectacles in one restless hand, and the round eyes that stared right at us, under heavy straight brows, were unmoving pools of dark.

"Mr. Holmes?" A deep level voice. "And Dr. Watson. I understand the countess sent for you to assist in this terrible business of the Thistle of Scotland."

"Quite correct, Mr. Stanley."

"Anything turn up yet?"

"Nothing too promising, I'm afraid."

Stanley gave a simultaneous short sigh and quick nod.

"You are not surprised?" Holmes asked.

"Certainly not. All likely places had been searched, thoroughly, before I left Mowbray House."

"You are positive the stone was in the clip when the breakfast began?"

"I am. I saw it as I seated myself."

"Can you name any later time when you are still certain that the stone was in place?"

Stanley ran his hands through his short hair in a gesture of exasperation. "I've been asking myself that, Mr. Holmes, and I can't answer. The clip fitted totally on the back of Lady Caroline's hair, you understand, and I was of course seated beside her. Once we were both sitting, I couldn't see the clip at all."

"The same would apply to the other guests?"

"It would, yes."

"When you rose to give the toast, I understand that you looked down at Lady Caroline?"

"I did. She had turned her head slightly away, and I suddenly realized that, while I could see the shape of the clip, I couldn't see the amethyst. So I leaned over a little, and," his mouth tightened, "the stone had gone."

"When you cried out, what did Lady Caroline do?"

"Pressed her hands to her face. She may have gasped. Probably she did. I really didn't notice."

"Did she say anything?"

"I don't think so. What was there to say?"

"And you, Mr. Stanley? What did you do?"

He gave a cold smile. "Acted like a fool, I'm ashamed to say. Just stood there, gaping, and dabbing at Lady Caroline's gown with my napkin. I'd spilled wine over her from the glass in my hand."

"What do you think has happened to the stone?"

"I've no idea."

"None at all?"

There was a short pause. "I know where I would look."

"Where, Mr. Stanley?"

"Among the servants."

"That is, I believe, being done."

"Good. I only hope it isn't too late." There was another pause, and then Stanley said slowly, "The real problem, of course, is that it is impossible that the amethyst could have been so loose in its setting that it would fall out. After all, the Thistle of Scotland had been in the hands of Manning of Gerrard's."

"And yet the amethyst has gone."

"So," Stanley agreed sarcastically, "I believe."

Ever since we had arrived, the sounds of movement, of drawers opening and closing, had come from an adjacent room. Now that door opened, and the elderly manservant entered. Stanley cast a quick eye on him. "Finished?"

"Yes, sir."

"Get the bags downstairs and find a cab."

"You're leaving, Mr. Stanley?" Holmes's brows rose, and I'm sure I looked astonished.

Certainly Stanley's distant expression became tinged with hostility. "Let us have no mistake, Mr. Holmes. I have explained matters to the American gentleman, and he has agreed to leave the sale of the Thistle of Scotland open until next Sunday. If the stone hasn't been found by then, steps will have to be taken to annul the marriage. It's damn inconvenient for me to be away from London right now, but it will be better for Lady Caroline's name if it is known that I am on the Continent. If I can do nothing further for you—"

"Lord Mowbray has your foreign address?"

"This," Stanley tapped an impatient finger on a folded sheet of paper on his desk, "notifies his lawyer."

"You are sending nothing to Lady Caroline?" I asked hotly, my indignation overcoming propriety.

Stanley turned his hard gaze on me. "My compliments." With which he rose and dismissed us with the shortest of bows. As we stepped out of the house onto the pavement, the elderly valet was putting the last bags into a waiting hansom.

"Poor Lady Caroline!" I exclaimed as soon as we were back in our own cab.

"One could say that Dolph Stanley is merely being honest," Holmes suggested.

"Then I despise honesty," I retorted.

To this Holmes made no answer, and, as we

---

turned back onto Oxford Street, I asked, "Was there anything remarkable about Lady Caroline's jewel case?"

"That depends on how you define the adjective, Doctor. The case has a very simple lock, so simple that I fear finding a key to open it would not be difficult." A distant clock chimed the hour. "Ten o'clock," Holmes noted with a sigh. "Too late for any further calls tonight, I fear. I'll get out at Baker Street, and you can keep the cab."

We rode for some moments in silence. Then I asked, "What did you pick up from the bathroom floor? I noticed nothing."

"This." Holmes took from his pocket a piece of white thread, perhaps three inches long.

I stared at it. "I can't see that that can be of any importance, Holmes. It's just an ordinary bit of thread."

"Where did it come from?"

"Why...who can say? Perhaps from the housemaid's apron when she mopped out the room."

"The thread is unlikely to have come from any apron," Holmes replied, "for it is not from woven material. It is thread from a spool and has been cut at both ends."

"Then it caught on the maid's apron when she was last sewing," I said impatiently, "and happened to drop off while she was cleaning the bathroom."

"No maid would wear the same apron when she was sewing that she had previously used for such tasks. Also, when washing a floor, you are moving backward in order not to tread on the wet area; the mop should therefore have removed anything dropped from the person."

"What is your theory, then?" I asked, feeling a little nettled at so much pother over a trifle.

———

"I don't yet have enough facts to form one," Holmes replied, "and am therefore that much ahead of Inspector Macready."

"You think he already has a theory?"

"The signs point that way. A theory that takes no account of this little piece of white thread." Holmes stowed it carefully away. "What did you make of Lady Caroline's having that gutta-percha toy in her pocket?"

"Perhaps a favourite childhood plaything, which in her state of shock she picked up without realizing what she was doing."

"The little head would seem to have been a much more recent purchase, for its price of one penny was still clearly written on it. Here we are at Baker Street. Shall I see you tomorrow, Watson?"

"Expect me in the early afternoon," I said.

Chapter IV

. . . Tangled in her hair
—Richard Lovelace,
To Althea: From Prison

The next morning I rose betimes and, taking a cab to hurry my progress, plunged into my day's calls. Those completed, I returned home to swallow a hasty luncheon and ask my neighbour to take afternoon surgery for me. Heading for Baker Street, I travelled through streets turned into a fairyland of glitter, leaves so crisp underfoot they crackled like starched shirt-fronts, and twigs of trees looking fat with frost against the clear sky.

Holmes was sitting late over his coffee, and I gladly accepted his offer of a cup. I had hardly settled into my old chair when from below came the ring of the bell.

Holmes cocked a quizzical eye at me as Mrs. Hudson was again heard on our stairs. "An Inspector Frederick Macready, sir," she announced.

"Show him up, Mrs. Hudson," Holmes said, "and bring another cup, if you'll be so kind. What will you wager, Watson, that our good inspector has come to tell us that the case is solved? Hark to his cock-a-doodle of victory."

"Something has roused his enthusiasm to fever pitch," I agreed, listening to the detective bound up two steps at a time. He burst into the sitting-room with a hearty cry of "Good morning!" and his deep-set eyes sparkled like the icy streets.

"Cold weather seems to suit you, Inspector," Holmes remarked.

"It's cold enough, in all truth." Macready tossed his hat and gloves onto a chair and began unwrapping the scarf that was wound nearly to his ears. "Coffee?" as Mrs. Hudson came in with the tray. "I'll take a cup with pleasure, for I won't deny that it's brutal outside. Brutal," he repeated, rubbing his hands together briskly, but for all that, satisfaction oozed from him like butter from hot muffins. "I can't stay long, Mr. Holmes—cream and three lumps, if you please—but I wanted to bring you up to date with this little affair of the missing amethyst."

You wanted to show off was my sour and silent comment.

"Now," the inspector took a quick gulp of his coffee, "three points were plain pretty well from the beginning. First, nobody *took* the stone directly out of the clip because nobody could have, not once Lady Caroline was sitting at the table. Second, that has to mean that someone had already loosened the setting—"

"What?" I exclaimed.

The inspector gave me a level look. "Can you think of any other way the deed could have been done?" I had nothing to offer, and Macready quickly continued, the note of triumph now strong in his voice. "The third point is that whoever stole the amethyst didn't care a brass farthing about the marriage because the marriage depends on the sale of that clip. So we don't need to waste time being so foolish as to worry about any of the family. You agree with me, Mr. Holmes?"

"I follow your reasoning."

"Of course you do," Macready replied, with a condescension that set my teeth on edge, "it's clear enough. Now as for the guests, none of 'em had any opportunity to get at the stone. Not," he added hastily, "that I would have suspected them in any case, but facts are facts, and none of them went near Lady Caroline after she sat down at the table. The two menservants, though—Rogers and that footman, Will Seeton—they of course were circling around and sliding in and out all the time."

"The kitchen staff—" I began.

Macready cut me off. "With the used dishes being taken off? Don't think I didn't have my eye on downstairs right from the start. Cook, kitchen girl, and two maids. No doubt all good at what they're trained to do and such forth, but I can tell you right out that none of 'em has the brains to run a neat little job like this amethyst caper.

"I'll grant that Essie Harris, the lady's maid, might, for she's a sharp little piece; fortunately for us she stayed upstairs the whole time, which means she's clear out of it. Nor, for I've been checking, has any of the women a single blemish on their reputations, nor any shady brothers, or undesirable followers, or anything of that nature. So we can forget about the women. That leaves Rogers and the footman." The inspector paused to take a couple more gulps of coffee.

"Rogers is unlikely to be the man we want," he resumed, "for he's been with the family for years, and as well is one of the leading lights of a little chapel out Bayswater way. But Will Seeton, he's a bit different. *Quite* a bit different is Seeton. He's only been with the family for about a year, and this is his first post of any kind."

This quick condemnation of a young lad on what seemed no evidence bothered me. "According to the accounts of the wedding we've heard," I said, "Seeton had no private access to the Thistle of Scotland, none at all. Or are you suggesting that more than one person was involved?"

"No, no." Macready shook his head vigorously. "There was one and one only, and that was Will Seeton. Here's how it was done. Mr. Torbram, Lord Mowbray's secretary, is proud as a peacock of that little scheme to guard the clip, and is sure no one downstairs except Rogers knew about it. But that's all nonsense. All the servants had learned that the clip was to be watched somewhere on that top floor by Mr. Torbram and Griffiths (a retired police officer, very sound chap). The staff mightn't have picked up the full details of the plan, but they knew that much, and a glance at that upper floor, with the table and two chairs set ready next to that old bathroom, would have told most of the rest."

The inspector went on with an outline of the events of the Saturday-evening dinner party, which agreed with what we had been told.

"Then," he continued, "once the guests had gone, Griffiths and Torbram took the jewel box, with the Thistle of Scotland locked in it, up to the top floor, parked it in the bathroom, and settled themselves at the table. What they *didn't* do is check any of those supposedly empty rooms up there, and Rogers, once he'd finished his own duties for the night, went to bed himself without looking in Seeton's quarters, off the kitchen." He paused and drained his cup, all the while eyeing us knowingly over the rim.

"You think that while Rogers was assisting Lord Mowbray to undress," Holmes asked, "Will Seeton slipped up the back stairs, and was already hiding in one of the unused bedrooms—"

"In that empty lumber room, Mr. Holmes, right next to the bathroom, and he was there before Griffiths and Mr. Torbram ever reached the top floor. Yes, I *will* have another cup of coffee, if you don't mind. I've really been too busy to have breakfast this morning."

"But," I objected, "how did Seeton obtain access to the Thistle of Scotland? There were two men on guard and a locked jewel box to bar his way."

"Well, now, Doctor, I don't know if you've ever had to keep a long watch in the cold and near dark, with nothing to do, nothing much even to think about?" I admitted that such experiences were not unknown to a doctor. "I'll warrant Mr. Holmes has too, so you'll both bear me out: after a couple of hours, it's just about impossible to keep yourself as alert as you were at the beginning."

"With that much I agree," Holmes replied succinctly. "So you think Seeton waited in that old lumber room until there was no sound from the watchers, then crept out—"

"Crawled out," Macready corrected, "on his hands and knees, to keep out of the light of the small lamp on the table. The door to the bathroom, where a candle had been left lit, was a bit ajar, so all Seeton had to do was ease himself in, open the box—"

"Which was locked," I again objected.

Macready gave a superior smile. "That kind of chap can open that sort of lock in his sleep."

"What kind of chap?" I insisted. "A footman in a respectable house?"

———

To this the inspector paid no attention. "Seeton loosened the setting of the amethyst, put the clip back, locked the box up again, slipped out the way he had come in, and made his way off downstairs."

"Why didn't he steal the amethyst then if that was his ultimate intention?" I demanded.

"He didn't dare, because of course it would have been found missing in the morning. With two chaps on guard who are really above suspicion, a hunt would have started that might easily have tripped Seeton up. How did he know that someone hadn't noticed he wasn't in his room when he was supposed to be? His plan was to let the stone fall out when there'd be a lot of people around."

"How did he know that the clip wouldn't be examined closely enough in the morning for the loose setting to be discovered?" I persisted.

"He could be pretty sure that it wouldn't be," Macready returned, "because, you see, the arrangements were that the jewel box wasn't to be brought downstairs until the last minute, when the family were waiting to leave for church. And of course everyone had had a good look at the clip the evening before; there was no reason they'd be wanting another."

"How did Seeton know when the stone would fall out?" Holmes asked.

Macready smiled delightedly. "He didn't; that was all part of his cleverness. As footman, you see, he knew he'd be at the family's back all the time: in the drawing-room before they left, all the way to and from the service, at the church, back again in the hall at Mowbray House, and of course then in the dining-room. He had a good chance of snatching the stone up unseen whenever it came out because of course he'd be the only one on the watch."

"But it did fall out, you think, during the breakfast," I said thoughtfully.

"I don't *think* it did, Dr. Watson," the inspector replied robustly, "I *know* it did. Well, we all do, for, if there's one thing that's clear, it's that the amethyst was in the clip in Lady Caroline's hair when the breakfast started and gone by the time it finished. What happened is that Lady Caroline nodded, or laughed a bit vigorously—with the marriage so important to the young lady, it's no wonder if she was in high spirits—and the stone slipped out, catching on her hair or maybe on the back of her gown. Seeton, being on the ready, snatched it up like that," Macready snapped his fingers, "while he was leaning over her shoulder, serving."

"And what did he do with it?" Holmes asked. "For he was searched, wasn't he? As were the rooms in which he was?"

The inspector finished his coffee and slowly set the cup down, obviously relishing our suspense. "He *swallowed* it," he finally replied and sat back, grinning. If my face matched my feelings I looked gratifyingly astonished, and even Holmes had widened his eyes. "Seeton anticipated the search, you see, so he popped the stone into his mouth and swallowed it."

Having succeeded in stupefying us, the inspector now rose and buttoned his coat. "I never left Seeton alone for one second after I sized up the situation, and if I do say so myself, that was pretty soon." He wrapped his scarf around his neck and reached for his hat and gloves. "I didn't leave Mowbray House until dawn, and I took Will Seeton with me. He's at the station now, and I expect he'll be charged before night."

"Will there be a policeman on guard at Mowbray House tonight?" Holmes asked.

"No, no, Mr. Holmes; no need for that now. We've got our man, and we'll soon have the amethyst too. There's such a thing as castor oil, you know." With a bright chuckle and a cheery nod, Inspector Macready bustled off.

"Well!" I exclaimed as his heavy steps bounced down the stairs. "What do you think of all that, Holmes?"

"The inspector's ideas are quite like some of your own, Doctor: ingenious but without much evidence to support them."

"You did say that the lock of the jewel box was a very simple one," I recalled, rather unwillingly. "Macready has at least taken note of that."

"Quite so. What, though, of the strange alteration to the setting of the clip? According to the inspector's theory, that should have been loosened. As he would have discovered if he had examined the clip with open mind and close sight, the opposite is true."

"Another failure of the inspector's," I suggested with mild sarcasm, "was not to discover those check trousers, that thread on the bathroom floor, and the rubbed bark of the plane tree. No doubt he also knows nothing of Lady Caroline's little toy head."

"''Tis true, 'tis pity, and pity 'tis 'tis true,' " Holmes quoted impishly. "Macready is also astray," he went on more seriously, "in assuming that Seeton hid in the lumber room; there is a skim of dust over the floor that is quite undisturbed. In fact, the only upstairs room besides the old bathroom that shows signs of recent entry is that one by the stairs."

"Where you found those old clothes?"

"Exactly. Nor is Macready correct in assuming

73

that Lady Caroline was in lively spirits during her wedding breakfast. I have spent the morning seeing some of the guests, including that astute lady, Mrs. Marshall, and all agree that Lady Caroline was so quiet as to seem sombre."

"I suppose it's possible that the amethyst had already somehow come out of the clip during the ride home from the church," I suggested, "and that it caught in Lady Caroline's hair so close to the clip that it seemed to be still in place."

"The only evidence I can think of that supports that idea," Holmes drained the coffee-pot into our cups, "is the fact that few of the wedding party or guests were young, and therefore that few can be expected to have good sight."

"That was what struck you about the list of guests?"

"It was, yes, and my assumption has been confirmed by the people I have seen so far. Even the groom needs spectacles, you'll have noted, and he naturally did not wear them for his wedding."

"When you asked Eustace Mowbray to compare the emerald of your tie-pin to the missing amethyst, I suppose you were really testing his eyesight?"

Holmes nodded. "Therefore we must bear in mind his positive statement that the amethyst was indeed in the clip in his sister's hair when she entered the dining-room immediately ahead of him. The stone was then 'glitterin' like a deuced drop of pink bubbly,' to use his own words."

"He could be lying, I suppose," I said slowly, "although at the moment I can't see why he should."

"Nor can I. Miss Powle remains another possible witness of value, for she too is young and entered the dining-room on Eustace's arm."

I mused for a moment. "Dolph Stanley was the one who gave the alarm."

"He was."

"In leaning toward Lady Caroline he spilled champagne over her."

"Which he then attempted to wipe up by dabbing at her gown with his napkin. Also true. You really don't like him, do you?"

"I think his behaviour has been that of a cad," I replied vigorously. "And of course he wasn't searched before he left Mowbray House, and he is no longer in Britain."

"Your theory doesn't explain how the stone came out of a tightened setting, nor how and why that alteration was made to the clip." Holmes rose. "I wonder if Lady Caroline would see me again before I visit Sam Griffiths."

"Shall I come with you?" I asked hopefully.

"I should be delighted if you can spare the time."

"I came prepared to do so," I replied and reached for my coat.

We were lucky enough to find a cab not far from Baker Street. As we trotted along Park Lane, Holmes observed, "I've put Wiggins and his fellow Irregulars onto watching Carrington Fitzgerald."

I had almost forgotten that errant Irishman's possible connection with the case. "Whatever do you hope to find, Holmes?"

"Whatever there is to learn. Another glimpse of that young lad in the loud check trousers would be hopeful."

"If that lad is Seeton, Wiggins will have no sight of him," I said thoughtfully.

"Quite so."

We said no more until we had crossed the bridge

———

and pulled up, among a litter of faded golden leaves from the plane tree, in front of Mowbray House, where Holmes again instructed our cab to wait. We were admitted by Rogers, so white and drawn as to look positively haunted, and casting a glance of loathing at the large official seals that Macready had left on the dining-room door. Asking to see Lady Caroline, we were told that she felt unable to face anyone and was remaining in her room.

"Understandable," Holmes observed sympathetically. "I hear that the footman, Will Seeton, has been detained by the police."

Rogers nodded. He really seemed unable to speak.

"That must have been a great shock for you."

"Terrible, sir," he whispered.

"Seeton was good at his duties? I believe he was the most recent addition to the household."

Rogers answered promptly enough; his voice, though, was very low, and his eyes wavered. "Will was young and inexperienced, sir, but learning. He handled himself very well at the wedding breakfast," the butler added defensively.

"Then we'll hope that he can quickly be released," Holmes replied soothingly, "for I'm sure that with such a small staff you must find it hard to do without his services. Now if I could have a word with Essie, we'll leave you in peace."

We were shown once more into the library, and there Essie quickly appeared. Since we had seen her on the previous day, her little face had become pale and strained, and she at once asked, "Is there any news about Will, sir?"

"None that I know of, Essie. What do you think of his detention?"

"He's innocent as I am, sir," she replied, with a challenging toss to her little chin.

"Then you won't mind helping me with my investigation?"

"That I won't, sir," she replied vehemently. "Donna be afeared of that."

"Could you show us that upstairs window that the plane tree touches, without our disturbing anyone?"

After a preliminary foray to make sure the coast was clear, Essie took us up the back stairs to the end of the second-floor hall. The window here was a casement that opened inward, fastened top and bottom with stout bolts.

These Holmes looked at closely. "I had wondered if anyone could have climbed in here," he explained to Essie with only partial truth, "but these bolts make all safe." As he spoke he was sliding the bolts back and forth; they ran with suspicious ease. "Thank you, Essie."

"You'll do what you can for Will, sir?" she asked pleadingly.

"We're trying to find the thief of Lady Caroline's amethyst, Essie."

"Yes, sir. Which'll free Will, because it isn't him."

"Sure of that, are you?"

"Ever so sure, sir."

"Why?"

She blushed. "I just am, sir."

Holmes surveyed her for a long moment of silence, but produced nothing more helpful than deeper blushes and downcast eyes. He then asked if he could see all of Lady Caroline's jewel boxes. Essie quickly brought four cases, the rosewood one that had been used to hold the Thistle of Scotland, a rectangular box of deep-rose leather, a round ebony container inlaid with mother-of-pearl, and a multi-drawer little case of papier mâché. Withdrawing the key from the leather case, Holmes tried it on the rosewood one; it fit perfectly.

"Where are all the cases kept, Essie?"

"In Lady Caroline's dressing table, sir."

"In a locked cabinet?"

"No, sir." Essie dropped her voice to a near whisper. "There's nothing more than a passel of trinkets in them, sir."

"Trinkets," Holmes repeated thoughtfully. "Including a toy gutta-percha head?"

Essie looked quite astonished. "Oh no, sir. Why would her ladyship have anything like that?"

That most certainly was a question that I at least couldn't answer. All Holmes said was "Thank you, Essie" and led the way out.

As we climbed back into our cab, he remarked, "Signs of a little romance between Essie and Will, do you think, Doctor?"

I did, though the topic wasn't of much interest to me at the moment. "The fact that the jewel box holding the Thistle of Scotland was locked is really meaningless, isn't it?"

"I'm afraid so. A key to open it would be absurdly easy to find."

"So Macready is at least right in treating the matter lightly. What of those bolts on that hall window? They seem to slide very easily."

"Because they have been recently oiled. What do you say to my thread-trousers-tree trilogy now?"

"That more data is required," I replied prudently, bringing a chuckle from Holmes. "We're going now to see Sam Griffiths, that retired policeman?"

"We are, off Tottenham Court Road."

Holmes had already settled into his corner, his head on his breast; obviously he was pondering some aspect of the case, and I could expect no further conversation for the moment. We crossed by Westminster Bridge, with its superb view of the parliament buildings, then travelled along the Victoria Embankment. The Grand Hotel on Northumberland Avenue made me resolve to take Mary to dinner there very soon, and a sight of the newly opened Garrick Theatre brought a question to my lips as to whether Holmes had yet attended. One glance at his still figure, and I went back to watching the passing scene, in London always changing, always fascinating. We paused for several minutes to allow a hearse, pulled by six black-plumed horses, to walk by, the crêpe-decorated mutes and two dozen carriages following. A hot-chestnut seller was engaged in a lively dispute with an apple woman, with a policeman complacently smoothing his moustache and tolerantly listening. Too soon for me we had turned down the shabby confines of Tottenham Court Road, and then off it to Garden Row.

We found Sam Griffiths in the end house of a terrace, ensconced with list shoes propped on a green frieze footstool drawn close to a glowing fire. A large brass clock and two candlesticks graced the mantel, a shiny horsehair sofa was well-covered with crocheted antimacassars, a Wilton rug was on the floor, a hooked mat lay before the hearth, and a comfortable aroma of kippers pervaded the room. In short, Sam Griffiths was surrounded by all the little comforts of an augmented pension, and he himself showed every sign of such enjoyment. Of above-average height, he was now of more than average plumpness, and his manner could only be described as well-satisfied.

Griffiths had of course heard of Holmes, and we were soon seated by the fire and served with good strong tea, brought in blue-and-white porcelain cups with silver spoons in the saucers by his smiling little wife, who bustled out of the kitchen for the purpose and as promptly retired again.

"I understand that you were hired to help guard the famous hair ornament known as the Thistle of Scotland, Mr. Griffiths," Holmes began.

"That's right, sir, and a 'orrible cold time of it we 'ad, up there on that top floor. But when you're paid for a job, you've no right to complain, and I will say that the cook put as good a breakfast in front of me in the morning as I've ever sat down to, and that's something you can't say for many places."

"Do you do much of such private duty now that you're retired?"

"Quite a bit, sir, for if I do say so myself, I 'ave a good name. Six-and-thirty year I was with the force, never a black mark against me, and twice letters of commend for being sharp-like when it was most needed. So I've let my name stand at the old station as willing to do these little jobs, and one tells another, you know, and so hardly a month goes by but I'm out 'elping somewhere. Guarding of the wedding presents is often what it is."

"Guarding of a different kind the night before last, I hear," Holmes observed genially, though I noted the keen watch being kept by those dark-grey eyes. "Did you see the Thistle of Scotland yourself?"

"In a manner of speaking I did, sir, for when the butler took me up to the drawing-room, 'is lordship 'ad a wooden box in 'is 'ands, a little thing it was," Griffiths' well-padded hands sketched a six-by-ten-inch shape, "and the lid was still open. And didn't that there stone shine!" Griffiths pursed his mouth in a soundless whistle. "Five thousand pound the papers say the Thistle of Scotland is worth, and after 'aving that one look, Mr. 'Olmes, I tell you I believe 'em."

"Lord Mowbray then locked the jewel box," Holmes prompted.

" 'E did, sir, and pocketed the key. Then 'e gave the box to Mr. Torbram—'e's 'is lordship's secretary—and 'e led the way up to that top floor. 'E takes the box into the bathroom and leaves it on the back of the commode chair, and we settle down at the table in the 'all. I'd worn my old police overcoat, and before the night was out I was right glad of it, I can tell you. Perishing it was up there, fair perishing."

"I'm sure it must have been," Holmes agreed heartily, "for it was certainly a bitterly cold night. You had a lamp, did you, on the table? Or a candle?"

"Both, sir. That is, Mr. Torbram took a lamp up with us and set that on the table, and then 'e lit a candle that 'ad been left ready on the wash-stand in the bathroom."

"Why wasn't the jewel box put on the wash-stand too?" I asked, for the incongruity of the glittering ornament it contained being left on the back of a commode chair offended me.

"I expect because, the candle being on the wash-stand, the commode corner was darker, like. So if any thief 'ad come peeking in, 'e'd 'ave 'ad to look all 'round afore 'e'd ever 'ave spotted that there box."

"What did you think of all these arrangements, Mr. Griffiths?"

He hesitated, obviously unsure whether it would be proper for him to criticize the ways of an earl's household. Holmes, however, gravely insisted that he wanted Griffiths' opinion as a man of much experience, and soon the retired officer's reserve melted into confidentiality.

———

"Well, sir, since you've asked I'll tell you. Things were a bit too fancy, like, for my taste. More frill than frock, if you take my meaning. Mr. Torbram says as 'ow Lord Mowbray was afraid someone'd guess the Thistle of Scotland was being kept in the 'ouse and try breaking in. That's sensible enough, far's it goes, for you can never tell just what the boys down Whitechapel way or 'round the Dials might know. More than you want, you can be sure of.

"But why figure any robber'd only try a window outside where the clip was being kept? What was going to stop 'em from breaking in downstairs somewhere? I'd 'ave set 'alf a dozen stout chaps in full uniform, bull's-eyes on the blaze, marching 'round outside the 'ouse all night, and damned any thief in London to try anything on. But there! Gentlemen 'ave their own ways of looking at things, and all went off like clockwork, I'll say that."

"Did you or Mr. Torbram go into the bathroom during the night?"

"Why, of course we did, Mr. 'Olmes. To use the offices, like."

"Did you try to lift the lid of the jewel box, by any chance, to have another look at the Thistle of Scotland? After all, you can't have many chances of seeing such an historic piece of jewellery."

Griffiths' eyes twinkled. "If the box 'adn't been locked, I'm not saying I mightn't 'ave took a peek. But I'd seen 'is lordship turn the key with my own eyes, so I wasn't what you'd call tempted."

"And there was no disturbance of any kind during the night?"

"Never a blessed thing," Griffiths replied with comfortable assurance. "What's all this about, Mr. 'Olmes, if you don't mind my asking?"

"The amethyst disappeared from the clip during

the wedding breakfast, Mr. Griffiths."

If ever a man looked thunderstruck, it was the retired officer. He froze in position, his eyes bulged, his mouth gaped, and, though his lips moved, all that came out was a series of gasps. Before he could recover and start a barrage of questions, we left.

"Griffiths knew nothing of the stone's disappearance," I said positively as the cab carried us back down Tottenham Court Road.

"I agree, Doctor, he did not. I wonder why he was chosen for the job."

"He has a good reputation, surely?"

"He has, for I asked at the station. However, the short list of retired officers recommended to Lord Mowbray included 'Dodge' Jackson. You remember him?"

"Very well," I replied, for I had encountered that thin fellow with the bulldog jaw on several of Holmes's earlier cases.

"I am wondering why anyone would choose Sam Griffiths over the Dodger."

"Perhaps Jackson was unavailable."

"Not so. He was even called to Mowbray House for an interview, as were Griffiths and two others. You can stay on the chase awhile longer, Doctor? Then let us call on Lady Caroline's bridesmaid, Miss Powle."

Though the Powle home was not in the best area of Mayfair, lying as it did off Vigo Lane, with its neighbours allowing it little room and the back of the Museum of Practical Geology its main view, the plain red brick Georgian building was far more pleasing than the jumbled architecture of Mowbray House. Inside we were led by an august butler up to the drawing-room, and there very soon Miss Powle joined us.

She was a short and plump young lady, with reddish hair bunched in wiry ringlets over each ear, tied with deep blue ribbon that matched the cording of her gown. "Mr. Holmes?" she began in a lofty manner most certainly copied from some more matronly figure.

He bowed. "Allow me to present Dr. Watson."

"How do you do, sir." With this Miss Powle's preternatural dignity fell away, and with a very girlish burst of anxious curiosity she asked, "Oh, Mr. Holmes, *is* there any news about Caroline's amethyst?"

"I'm afraid not, Miss Powle, and that is why we are here. I understand that you were the bride's attendant, and so were of course at the supper party on the night before the wedding." Holmes went on with simple, direct questions that took Miss Powle through the events of that evening and of the following morning. For some time we heard nothing new and nothing, to me at least, at all helpful.

As for the search of Lady Caroline's hair and clothing, Miss Powle was emphatic that it had been very thorough.

"Lady Caroline wore her hair in a chignon, I understand," Holmes observed.

Miss Powle nodded. "The countess had wanted Essie to make a nest of ringlets, as she did for the dinner the evening before, but somehow the curl papers had come out during the night. When I arrived yesterday morning, Caroline's hair was all hanging down, straight as ever, and all Essie could do was pin it up in the nape of Caroline's neck as usual. And after all," Miss Powle added, "the ornament looked lovely, even if it had to be rather... *perched*, you know, on top of the chignon, not set into the curls the way it was for the dinner party."

———

"I'm sure the effect was charming even without the ringlets. I understand the amethyst is very large."

"Very."

"Is it much bigger than this stone?" Holmes had once more taken out his emerald tie-pin and was holding it up, some six feet from Miss Powle.

"I . . . I think so. I really don't. . . ." She leaned forward, squinting just a trifle. Holmes too leaned forward, slowly advancing his hand toward the young lady. When it was within two feet of her eyes, Miss Powle exclaimed, "Oh, now I see it! Oh, the amethyst is ever so much larger than that, Mr. Holmes. You *will* find it for Caroline, won't you? It means so much to her."

"We're certainly doing our best," Holmes assured our little hostess. We made our farewells and left.

When we were again in a cab I observed, "Miss Powle is very short-sighted."

"Yes."

"So the only person of the whole party who had good eyes was Eustace Mowbray. He says he is certain that the amethyst was in its right place when Lady Caroline entered the dining-room."

Holmes said nothing until we were heading up Regent Street. Then he finally murmured, "It *is* strange. As yet I can see no explanation."

"I'm not surprised," I said with a sigh. "That the amethyst should disappear before twenty people—"

"I was referring to Lady Caroline's hair."

"Her hair!"

"You do not think it strange that a young lady's curls should come loose from their moorings on the night before her wedding, a time when she would surely wish to look her best?"

"Probably she spent a very restless night," I replied. "Not at all uncommon before a wedding, I assure you."

"Ask Mrs. Watson if a restless night would so disarrange hair papers put in by a lady's maid, especially as the papers put in the previous night apparently remained firmly in place. And then there is that little gutta-percha head. . . . You have to leave me, Doctor? Yes. And I must see the rest of the wedding guests and put some inquiries in motion too. Until tomorrow then, Watson."

Chapter V

To lay their just hands on that golden key
—John Milton,
Comus, line 13

A medical man in active practice never has perfect control over how he spends his time. Early on Tuesday morning I was urgently summoned to Sussex Street, and had to stay for over three hours before I was satisfied that no untoward event threatened the safety of my patient. Then, as I started the day's calls, I was confronted by the cacophony of coughs and wheezes which cold weather so often brings to London, and ordered a virtual acre of mustard plasters and a gallon of friar's balsalm. When I at last headed for my old lodgings on Baker Street, all the church chimes warned me that one o'clock was striking.

To my surprise I found Holmes still in his dressing-gown and just starting on a plate of excellent kedgeree. "You are breakfasting late," I remarked. "Thank you, Mrs. Hudson," for the considerate woman had followed me up the stairs with a cup of coffee, "that will be very welcome. Though I believe the weather is at last moderating."

"I certainly hope so," Holmes replied, "for I had a cold time of it last night. I was watching Mowbray House."

"Whatever for, Holmes?"

"Because after the amethyst's disappearance, the police were both inside and out from noon until dawn. So last night was the first opportunity for anyone to—"

"Climb the plane tree, no doubt in those check trousers," I interrupted, with an exasperated smile, "in order to drop another three-inch length of thread on the bathroom floor and then to disorder Lady Caroline's hair papers."

Holmes answered the last part of my jest seriously. "Lady Caroline's hair papers were an unusual addition to her evening toilette, put in so that she would have ringlets to frame the Thistle of Scotland, and therefore their disruption is a possible clue. If I didn't discover anything about that, I did find one further fact last night: someone else is interested in Mowbray House after dark. I had my hansom leave me by the Archbishop's Park so that I could look about me while I approached. As I turned onto Mowbray Crescent, a small and well-dressed man with a goatee hurried off."

"A mere passer-by," I suggested.

"Hardly, for within ten minutes he came cautiously back, and, as I kept myself well out of sight, began pacing up and down along the Crescent. I finally let him have a glimpse of me, and he once more quickly shied away, only minutes later to creep back and return to his walking vigil."

"He knew you?"

"Not in my persona of an old man with a stick, hobbling around a distant corner."

"You have no idea who he was?"

Holmes shook his head. "As far as I know, I have never seen him before."

"What could he have wanted? If his purpose were honest, why not go openly to the house?"

"All I can yet say is that his path kept the bed-chambers of the family—and of Essie Harris and Wade Torbram—in steady view, and that he left the area some half-hour after the last light, that of Lady Caroline's room, had been extinguished." Holmes pushed back his empty plate and stretched. "My guard duty produced another interesting fragment of information. A little after eleven o'clock Eustace left Mowbray House, shutting the front door very gently after him; except for scuttling into the shadows, my fellow watcher paid him no attention. Some three hours later Eustace returned, entering the house the same way and in the same cautious fashion."

"Perhaps he was merely being considerate of the distressed nerves of the household."

"Possibly. By the way, I have picked up a few details about the young man. Colonel Brice tells me that Eustace has had a rather unsatisfactory record ever since Eton. He attended Oxford, where he was much better at accumulating debts than knowledge. With great financial hardship, Lord Mowbray paid these and bought his errant son a commission in the Queen's Regiment."

"I cannot see that young man as a soldier, Holmes."

"Neither could he, or the Queen's. Within a few months Eustace left, by then owing several hundred pounds to his fellow officers beyond what the sale of his commission brought. Since that time he has undergone a certain reformation, for he is now staying away from all the more dangerous forms of gambling, and is steadily winning a little at the clubs: apparently those slim hands have a real skill with cards. Colonel Brice thinks that Eustace might now drift along well enough if his father could once more pay what his son owes and forget the past, but his lordship won't be inclined to do either should he learn the truth."

"Yet if Eustace doesn't soon clear his debts of honour, he will no longer be welcome at the clubs."

"Caught in a nice dilemma, isn't he? Certainly he needs to stay in London, and therefore seems to have a strong reason to wish for his sister's marriage: as he said, that could give him a free home once Mowbray House is rented." Holmes drained his cup. "After you left me yesterday, I called on the rest of the wedding guests."

"Did you learn anything new?"

Holmes shook his head. "Only repeated confirmation of what we have already been told: that the Thistle of Scotland was shining in Lady Caroline's hair in all its glory when she sat down at the breakfast table, that no one except Rogers and Seeton went near her during the meal, and that therefore it's a total mystery what could have happened to the amethyst. Hark, what have we here?" For the downstairs bell had given a brisk peal.

Once more Inspector Macready was announced. He entered with a wide smile gleaming above the loose folds of his scarf. "Just stopped by to tell you the latest, Mr. Holmes. Morning, Doctor. Not quite as cold, is it?" He tossed off his overcoat. "We've been looking into the background of Will Seeton, and what do you think? He's from the bottom of Notting

Hill Road—born and bred into crime, you might say! Grew up with as tough a bunch of young thugs as you'd wish to see, and since the Mowbray family has come back to London, he's been spending his half-days larking around with his old pals."

"Has he ever been convicted of anything?" Holmes inquired.

The inspector gave a lofty smile. "No, no, Mr. Holmes; chaps like young Seeton are a mite too fly to be caught that easily. But he was chums with a lad whose brother runs with the Clogger gang. You won't have heard of Clogger, but—"

"He is chief of a dozen young hoodlums who use the Leather Bottle as headquarters," Holmes interrupted. "Their chief livelihood comes from small thefts from the shops of the area, though since Clogger's present girl has a sister married to a dockyard navvy, petty pilfering occasionally also ends up in the back room of the Leather Bottle."

Macready looked somewhat taken aback by Holmes's knowledge of London's minor underworld. "That's the chap. What's more, Rogers knew of Seeton's background when he hired the fellow! A fellow with no experience as a footman! What do you think of that?"

"Unusual."

"I should think so!" The inspector had posted himself, unbidden, in front of the fire and now lifted his coat-tails with clasped hands. "That a butler who's supposed to be a rock of rectitude would take a young varmint like Seeton into his master's household, and that master an earl too... Why, it beggars all. We've got Rogers down at the station now, so I'd better get back to it."

"How did Seeton respond to the castor oil?" Holmes asked demurely.

———

"We haven't used it yet, Mr. Holmes. We're patient, you know, very patient." With a knowing nod Macready had gone.

"Well, well." Holmes paused thoughtfully. "The inspector is certainly trying to build a case. Perhaps Essie does have reason to be concerned for her Will."

"Is the Clogger gang of such notoriety?"

"Most of them are nothing more than public-house braggarts, but Clogger himself has enough intelligence to aim higher."

"As high as the Thistle of Scotland? That would surely be uncommon."

"It would, yes, though no more so than for a lad from the lower purlieus of Notting Hill to become a footman in an earl's household. Speaking of unsavoury aspects of London life, during my forays yesterday I picked up a little news of Fitzgerald. His debts are at an all-time high, and his creditors are holding back only because of the imminent death of his uncle. Though the old man still refuses to see Fitzgerald, he certainly favoured him at one time, and hope springs eternal in the breasts of both debtors and creditors."

"No sign of that young chap in the check trousers?"

"Wiggins has found none."

"And Seeton is still in gaol," I said significantly.

Holmes made no reply, his thoughts obviously elsewhere. "I must go out, but I had better return quickly," he said at last. "Rogers may seek me when he is released from the station."

"You don't suppose the inspector will arrest him too?"

"I doubt if even Macready will go that far at this

stage. You must be off as well, Doctor? Then dine with me tonight."

This I readily promised to do, and so we parted.

When at six o'clock I returned to Baker Street, Rogers had not appeared. He arrived, though, not long after we had risen from the table. One glance at the wretched man, and Holmes reached for the brandy.

"I am not a drinker, sir," the butler began, his trembling lips hardly able to form the words.

"Let me take your coat and hat," I said firmly, "and sit here by the fire. Now sip this glass and wait a few minutes before you try to speak."

He did so, and a little colour slowly flowed back into his drained face. "I have been questioned at the police station," he said in a low voice, as if this in itself were an admission of terrible guilt.

"So Inspector Macready informed us earlier. What did he want from you?"

"Everything I know about Will Seeton." Rogers shut his eyes at the memory of his ordeal.

"I'm afraid that is quite normal under the present circumstances."

"The trouble is, Mr. Holmes, that nearly everything I know about Will is to his discredit. Yet I still believe... At least I am striving to believe..."

"In his innocence?"

"As far as the theft of the amethyst is concerned, Mr. Holmes, yes. Innocence in the true and total sense is, I fear, beyond Will, though it breaks my heart to have to admit it."

Rogers' story was simple enough. His sister had married a man who had a small shop half-way up Notting Hill Road. One of their customers was Will's mother, a poor rag of a woman with a drunken dust-man for a husband and half a dozen starveling children. While visiting his sister, Rogers had met Will, and invited him to a little social gathering at the chapel. To his pleased surprise, Will not only turned up, but thereafter not infrequently attended such events, and though no doubt his chief interest was in the refreshments, Rogers was encouraged to hope for better things for the boy.

"What lads like Will need more than anything else, sir," the butler went on, "is good honest work well away from their old neighbourhoods and companions. When Lord Mowbray and the family left London at the end of last season, we lost our footman. He had been dissatisfied for some time, for the wages are low—very low, I might even say—and country living isn't ever popular with young fellows. I couldn't find an experienced man at the price, Will was much on my mind, and I thought I'd have time to train him properly before we returned to London. He jumped at the chance, which I thought a good sign, and as long as we were down in Kent, all went well enough.

"Of course Will is small in stature for a footman, and at first he knew nothing, truly nothing, of what would be expected of him. His manners were deplorable, and as for his speech, you could hardly understand two words out of ten, and those you didn't want the women to hear. But he was eager, smart like a monkey, and he was learning very quickly. I even thought that, with some quiet help from me, Will might be able to be part of Lady Caroline's household, for Mr. Stanley lives in Bloomsbury and would be doing very little entertaining."

"Lady Caroline was going to live on that little street off Rathbone Place?" I asked, a dismal memory of that ill-fashioned, ill-furnished house very clear in my mind.

"She was, sir; Mr. Stanley owns the property, I believe. All went well with Will as long as I had him in the country; the trouble began when we returned to London. Of course Will has been visiting his family on his half-days, which is only proper, but I'm afraid he has also begun seeing some of his old companions in that area. On occasion he's been late returning, and more than once there has been beer on his breath. Worse, he was getting inattentive about his duties, nothing I said seemed to have any effect on him, and now this!" The poor butler sank his grey head onto his hands and groaned.

"Probably Seeton would be better to look for different work in the future," I said, thinking of Essie's unwise interest in him, "even if he is innocent of the theft of the amethyst."

"The future of his soul is what I'm concerned about, Dr. Watson," Rogers replied heavily. "It is for that that I've struggled. If Will has rewarded my efforts by betraying the trust that I know I should not have placed in a boy from such a background..."

"Let us at least begin by assuming him innocent," Holmes said encouragingly. "You and he together served the wedding breakfast, I believe?"

"We did, sir. It was really too large a party for the two of us to handle alone, but the parlourmaid is elderly and inclined to become flustered, and my lord refused to have anyone hired. So Will and I did the whole meal, and I must say that he behaved well. In fact, as soon as we knew of the wedding plans he seemed very keen—"

"Did he!" I involuntarily exclaimed.

"He did, sir," Rogers replied defensively, "and I was most pleased to see it. In fact, the more I drilled him beforehand, the happier he seemed to be. 'Do it like this, Mr. Rogers?' he'd say. 'Like this? I'm getting the hang of it, aren't I, Mr. Rogers?' And he was, he was. When I think that it may all have been part of a deep and wicked plot..."

"Do you believe that?" Holmes asked quietly. "You, who know him better than anyone else in the house?"

For a moment Rogers closed his eyes, and his lips moved as if in prayer. Then out came the secret that Inspector Macready's most persistent questioning hadn't brought to light.

After the last course of the breakfast had been served, Rogers had briefly left Will alone in the dining-room while he checked that all was well in the kitchen. When he returned upstairs, the toasts were underway, and Will was going down the table with the champagne bottle, quite as he should have been. Taking advantage of this interval in his duties, Rogers made up the fire, which took him directly behind Lady Caroline, seated as she was in the place of honour at the table. As Rogers straightened from his task, his eyes fell on the shining silver of the thistle clip in his young mistress's hair. To his total consternation, he realized that the setting was empty.

"How good are your eyes?" Holmes asked.

"I am a little short-sighted, sir, but not so much that I wouldn't have been able to see a stone of that size when I was no more than a dozen feet from it."

"Could the jewel have been caught in Lady Caroline's hair or gown without your noticing it?"

"I don't believe so, sir, for I was that stupefied that I stared and stared, and moved around a bit still staring."

"How long was this before Mr. Stanley rose to give his toast and exclaimed that the stone had gone?"

"No more than two or three minutes."

"When was the last time that you are sure that you saw the amethyst?"

The butler gave a weary shake of the head. "I've asked myself that over and over, Mr. Holmes. Inspector Macready has done the same. All I can say to you is what I said to him: I don't know. The stone was in the clip at the beginning of the breakfast, I am sure of that, but I was soon too busy to pay any further attention to it."

"You have heard the inspector's theory? That Seeton hid in that old lumber room upstairs, crept unseen into the bathroom, loosened the amethyst so that it would fall out, and then watched his chance to pick it up, happening to do so while he served at breakfast?" The butler nodded. "What is your opinion?"

"It's hardly for me to say, sir."

"Can you say that the inspector's theory is definitely impossible?"

Rogers hesitated. "I think it most unlikely that anyone could have got past Mr. Torbram and that retired police officer unnoticed. But what is even more dead against the idea, if you understand me, sir, is Will himself. He isn't up to the scheme, not to thinking of it, nor yet to taking the risk, all without turning a hair."

"I see. Who in the Mowbray household has keys to the outside doors?"

"Keys, sir?" Rogers looked quite startled at the change of subject. "I do, to both the back and front. Lord Mowbray has to the front, not as far as I know to the back. That is all."

"Mr. Eustace doesn't have a key?"

"Not now," Rogers replied briefly.

"He did have one?"

"He did, Mr. Holmes, but after the season last year Lord Mowbray decided that that wasn't wise."

"I see. Who has that key now?"

"His lordship, and it doesn't leave his key ring."

"If Mr. Eustace is going to be out late, what are the arrangements?"

"The arrangements," Rogers replied austerely, "are that Mr. Eustace is *not* to be out late. If he isn't back by eleven o'clock, I wait up for him."

"And report the matter the next day to his lordship?"

"Such are my instructions, Mr. Holmes."

"You lock and chain both front and back doors before you retire at night?"

"I do, unless his lordship is out. Then he chains the front door after he has come in." The butler passed a trembling hand over his face. "Mr. Holmes, what am I to do?"

"Go home and eat your supper, and then retire to an early bed. You did well to come to me; you can do no more for the moment."

"And that poor boy?"

"He won't come to any great harm where he is. Or at least not to greater harm than that contained in two ounces of castor oil."

Rogers rose heavily. "I will remember him in my prayers."

"You have cause," Holmes answered quietly but made no other comment, and our visitor went slowly off downstairs.

"Rogers is demonstrably wrong on one point," I then said. "Eustace does have a key to the front door."

"At least he had one last evening. And in the face of Rogers' positive assertion that the young man's key was taken from him over a year ago, one wonders where he has obtained it."

"If a copy were made, would it be from Rogers' key or Lord Mowbray's?"

"I doubt Rogers' keys ever leave his possession, night or day. Lord Mowbray probably places his on the dressing-table at night, and, provided that they are there when he is ready to leave his room the next day, never thinks more of them."

"And as his lordship hasn't a valet, attending to his personal needs—hanging up his clothes, brushing his trousers, polishing his shoes—has surely been one of the tasks of the footman. Of none other than Will Seeton."

"My reasoning exactly, Doctor."

"Holmes," I said slowly, "that young fellow in the check trousers whom we saw cavorting on the street with Fitzgerald: he was about Eustace Mowbray's size, wasn't he?"

"Approximately, yes. Certainly shorter and much slighter in build than Fitzgerald."

"If Eustace at that time didn't have a key, could he have used those old clothes both as a disguise and to keep from damaging his own attire while he climbed down—and later up—that plane tree? The elation we saw being expressed by all that laughing and dancing around could have been caused by Fitzgerald's having successfully planned a way for Eustace to steal the amethyst."

Holmes gave one of his small smiles. "At least you are now taking those old clothes and that tree more seriously. Just what was Fitzgerald's scheme for obtaining the stone?"

I had to admit that I had no idea.

"I think," Holmes said, getting to his feet and

reaching for his coat, "that the time has come for me to pay a visit to Will Seeton. You can come with me, Doctor? Excellent."

We were fortunate in finding a cab before we had reached Oxford Street. As we headed toward the Thames, I asked Holmes if Wiggins had yet found out anything about Fitzgerald.

"That he has rooms on Oxender Street."

"Good Lord!" I exclaimed in disgust, for that was an area of "houses of accommodation" where rooms could be rented by the hour.

"Quite so. Fitzgerald emerges only in the evenings, which he spends in—shall we say—most varied ways. It's a good thing my Irregulars haven't led exactly sheltered lives. This is my second trip across the river today," Holmes added as we started across Vauxhall Bridge, "for after you left me this afternoon, I again went to Mowbray House. Lady Caroline was said to be lying down and not to be disturbed."

"I don't think you will learn anything more from her, Holmes. What could she possibly have to contribute?"

"Whatever she has not yet told us."

"You feel there is anything of importance?"

"Ah, that is more than I can yet say."

As we turned down Kennington Lane I told Holmes that I had asked my wife about the loss of Lady Caroline's hair papers. "Mary," I had to report, "thinks it most unlikely that the most restless of nights would make properly put-in papers come out, especially as almost surely a net or cap of some kind would have been worn over them."

"I agree with Mrs. Watson," Holmes replied, "and remain convinced that we will find the explanation before this case is over. Then there is the matter of that little gutta-percha head..."

"We call them gutta-percha," I offered idly, "but they aren't rubber. They're made from treacle and glue."

"Really? How do you happen to know that?"

"Because I once had a very young patient who had consumed the better part of one."

"I doubt that Lady Caroline intends eating hers," Holmes said drily as the cab slowed down and pulled to the curb. "Station-houses are never very prepossessing, are they?"

This one certainly was not, being a mere grey concrete block with a minimum of small windows and a single unadorned door framed by flaring gas lamps. Inspector Macready was not at the station, but Holmes knew the sergeant on duty. We were quickly shown into a small inner room, with a table, a few chairs, and a strong smell of carbolic, and there Seeton was soon brought.

He was about eighteen years old and, as Rogers had said, small for a footman, of the slight build that is so often the result of slum living, with straight brown hair now falling over his face, wide cheekbones, and a narrow and boyish chin. He had been taken in his livery, which had become sadly crumpled, and had been provided with neither clean linen nor the services of a barber. All in all, the mark of the gaol was already on him, and his truculent posture, sitting as he was with hunched shoulders and hanging head, emphasized it.

Holmes surveyed him for a moment and then said bluntly, "Inspector Macready believes that you are guilty of stealing Lady Caroline's amethyst."

"S'pose that's news to me?" the young man

snapped without looking up. "Yer daft enough to think so yerself, I 'spect." His belligerent speech showed traces of Rogers' recent teaching, overlapping the accents of lower London.

"I deal with facts," Holmes returned. "Prove to me that you're innocent, and I'll prove it to the inspector."

"I've told the per-lice everythin' I knows," Seeton muttered sulkily, "and a fat lot of good it's done me, 'asn't it?"

"Then what's the harm in telling your story again?"

Seeton considered this and finally conceded, though sullenly, that he had nothing further to lose. "Wot yer want to know, then?"

Holmes began with the little dinner party on the evening before the wedding. Seeton said he had shown in the jeweller from Gerrard's, who had been accompanied by "a big 'usky" who had waited in the hall. The pair were in the house only moments, and were let out by Seeton. By the time he returned to the drawing-room, the velvet case was open and being passed from one to another, rousing many exclamations of admiration. Then, as Rogers announced supper, Miss Powle took the clip out of the case and fastened it in Lady Caroline's hair.

After dinner, as soon as the guests had gone, Rogers sent Seeton and the women servants to bed; the footman thus hadn't witnessed the final preparations for the safekeeping of the clip. He did freely admit, however, that he, like the other six of the staff, had learned about the plan, although he denied knowing any of the specific details.

Holmes then passed on to the next morning. The staff had been roused early by the indefatigable Rogers. After a quick breakfast in servants' hall, the butler had gone up to assist Lord Mowbray to dress while Seeton attended Eustace, and then Rogers had sent the footman up to the top floor to tell Torbram and Griffiths that their watch could end.

"Did you see Mr. Torbram go into the bathroom for the jewel box?" Holmes asked.

"Yerse, but I never waited to see 'im come out. I just picked up the tray, and—"

"What tray?" Holmes's expression had instantly become intent.

"The tray that 'ad 'eld the lunch for Mr. Torbram and that old per-liceman."

"They had a lunch, did they?"

Seeton nodded. "Bein' as 'ow it was such a cold night and all. Mrs. Grogan 'ad got it ready afore she went to bed and left it on the lower landing."

"What was on the tray?"

"A plate of sangwidges and one of little cakes and tarts and a big pot of coffee. And a spirit burner to 'eat the coffee up because they wouldn't be 'avin' it for a while. Cups and saucers and such."

"Cream and sugar, no doubt?" Seeton agreed. "Was the tray Mrs. Grogan's idea, or did someone ask her to prepare it?"

"I dunno rightly which, but it wouldn't likely be Mrs. Grogan. She's not the kind to suggest things. Maybe it was part of the deal, like, with that old bobby. 'E looked as if 'e didn't go long without takin' a bite of summat."

"When you took the tray downstairs, had both cups been used?"

"They 'ad that. All the coffee'd gone, the food too, and the burner'd been lit, prob'ly more'n once. It was near empty anyways."

Holmes then took Seeton through the events of the wedding and the breakfast, but, except for such personal details as how "crool cold" it had been riding on the outside of the hired carriage, we learned nothing new. As to the precise time Seeton had himself last seen the amethyst, he insisted he couldn't be sure.

"I was that busy, see, and Mr. Rogers, 'e'd give me near more orders'n I could 'andle. But everythin' went off real good, I never spilled nothin', not so much as a drop, nor got mixed up. When Mr. Rogers went down the table with the powpats, I was right at 'is elbow with the brown sorce. That's why 'e let me take the champagne 'round while 'e popped down to the kitchen: 'e knew I could do it. And I did, just as good's 'e could 'ave. And then, just as I gets to the end of the table, Mr. Stanley jumps up and yells, and before I knows wot's wot, the per-lice 'ad come, and before yer could turn 'round, I'm landed 'ere. And 'ow could I 'ave stole 'er ladyship's joo-el? Plain imposs'ble, innit?"

Holmes didn't answer this. Instead he asked, "How much have you been seeing of your old friends at the Leather Bottle?"

"I been goin' there reg'lar on my 'alf-days," Seeton replied, promptly and defiantly, "*and* I 'as a glass of beer while I'm there. Wot of it? Think I'm goin' to ask for lemonade? And maybe I 'ears of a few goin's-on some of the lads 'ave been up to, or are thinkin' of startin', that that there inspector wouldn't like. Wot's that to me? *I* ain't takin' no part in 'em, am I? But I ain't spillin' on old pals neither."

"I'd think the worse of you if you would" was Holmes's calm reply.

"Yer would?" Seeton's scowling face cleared magically. "Then . . . yer believe me, sir?"

"I think you've told me the truth. Are you sure you've nothing to add?" The young fellow looked down and shifted his feet without answering. "Would you like to send a message to Essie?"

"That I would, sir!" He seemed, however, to have great difficulty in phrasing his message, and finally mumbled, "Tell 'er... tell 'er I'm thinkin' 'bout 'er. Thinkin' 'bout 'er all the time."

With that we left him.

"Well, Doctor," Holmes asked as we climbed into yet another cab, "what do you think of Will Seeton?"

"I agree with Rogers," I replied. "Seeton is far from ideal material for the post of footman in an earl's house, yet there is something likeable about the lad."

"Could he have concocted Macready's scheme for the theft of the amethyst?"

"No," I said emphatically. "Rogers is right there: Seeton isn't up to it."

"Could he have played a part in such a scheme?"

That caused me a long moment of thought. "I don't know," I had to conclude.

"Nor do I. What do you think about that lunch that was left for Torbram and Griffiths?"

"It seems strange that neither of them, nor Rogers, mentioned it."

"They may not have considered it important enough to do so," Holmes replied, "though it is certainly a matter that we will have to discuss with Sam Griffiths. *Nous verrons.* I'll get out here, for it is time I took up my watch on Mowbray House. Until tomorrow, Watson."

Chapter VI

The desideratum of a volume
—Charles Lamb,
*Detached Thoughts on
Books and Reading*

On Wednesday, having postponed most of my calls until the afternoon, I arrived at Baker Street around ten o'clock and found Holmes just leaving.

"Good morning, Doctor. Yes, we'll keep the cab, for another attempt to see Lady Caroline is the first item on my schedule. And I must deliver Will's message to Essie."

I was as uneasy about Holmes's acting as go-between for those young people as I was about his persistent wish to interview Lady Caroline again. "I suppose you also intend checking that plane tree for fresh signs of climbing?"

"I did that last night, without finding any. As for the rest of my vigil, Eustace was the only member of the household to go out during the evening. Once more he left, very quietly, at a little after eleven and returned, as noiselessly, between two and three this morning."

"Did the little man with the goatee appear?"

"He did, arriving a little before seven and leaving shortly after the last lights went out, at about ten-thirty."

I could make nothing of this and said as much, adding, "I really don't know what you're watching Mowbray House for, Holmes."

"Nor do I, Doctor, except to find out such facts as the mysterious stranger's interest in it and Eustace's discreet comings and goings. I am going to put my Irregulars on the trail of both tonight."

"Has seeing Will Seeton modified your opinion of the inspector's theory?" I asked as we once more crossed Vauxhall Bridge.

"Macready is certainly making too much of what he labels Seeton's criminal background: he is only finding what he was looking for. If the young man had turned out to be a stalwart of the chapel, no doubt our good inspector would have declared him a master of deception."

"Yet surely criminal association *is* important," I argued.

"If mere association is worthy of note, Doctor, who more guilty than Inspector Macready himself?"

"Really, Holmes! The purpose of the associa-tion—"

"Exactly, Doctor, exactly. Therefore the question is whether, since his return to London, Seeton has been visiting his Leather Bottle chums for auld lang syne, as he says, or to keep abreast of the Clogger lads' fencing knowledge." As we pulled up at Mow-bray House, Holmes said, "Since this is only the first call I must make, we'll have the cab wait. I don't think we'll be here long."

He was quite right: Rogers gave us the surprising news that Lady Caroline had gone to Mrs. Marshall's charity rooms on Millbank Street.

———

"Millbank Street!" I exclaimed, a picture of that unsalubrious industrial area flashing into my mind.

"And Horseferry Road," Rogers replied gloomily, adding that Lady Caroline was one of a group of young ladies who assisted Mrs. Marshall in giving aid to the poor.

"No doubt Lady Caroline will benefit from having some occupation," Holmes said tactfully. "She has gone alone?"

A slight frown of unease crossed the butler's brow. "She has, sir. Usually Mr. Eustace escorts her, but as no one expected Lady Caroline to wish to attend today, he had already gone out himself. The countess is resting, having been so much disturbed of late, and I didn't think it right to bother her. Of course I whistled for a four-wheeler, and saw that Lady Caroline had sufficient money with her for the fare. She should be perfectly safe."

"Oh, certainly. Tell her we called and hope to see her on another occasion. Now if we could have a word with Essie."

We were once more shown into the library, there to wait for several minutes. Holmes spent the time prowling through the scant and scattered contents of the shelves.

"Mr. Torbram is correct," he commented, "nothing here is of value either for rarity or condition. Indeed, there seems to have been deliberate damage done to some of the books. Look at this." He held out a folio, sermons of some unremembered divine that the last century had unwisely favoured with publication. Only the first pages had even been cut, yet a three-inch section of the handsome crimson leather had gone.

"However could that have been torn off?" I asked.

"Not torn, Watson: scissors have been the instrument." Holmes was using his lens on another book, a fat little collection of someone's adventures in Palestine, poorly bound and now quite dilapidated: two inches of its wine cloth cover had been slashed away. "And what have we here?" Holmes had pulled out a thin edition of poems in an ugly purple paper binding, a section of which had been sliced off. "Now this is something different." Holmes was peering through his glass at still another book, bound in deep blue, that to me looked undamaged. "There appears to be a faint stain on the spine, see it?" Now I could. "What's more," Holmes added, moving along the shelves, "the same discoloration shows here, and here, and yet here. How exceedingly odd." He paused, and his eyes held the hard dry glitter that invariably mark his moments of keenest interest.

His concentration was broken by Essie's entrance. The poor girl was certainly showing the strain of these unhappy days at Mowbray House, for her eyes were swollen, her expression deeply anxious, and, even as she dropped her dutiful curtsy, she burst out, "Can't you do something to help poor Will, sir? He's innocent, really and truly he is."

"If he is, Essie, I am sure—"

"He is, sir. Indeed he is! Oh, what can I do to make people believe me?"

"The best thing any of us can do is to find who is guilty."

"Yes, sir. But it's still Will who's in gaol, sir."

"I know, Essie. We saw him there last evening and have brought a message for you." To my surprise, her cheeks paled at this, and her lips tightened, almost as if her anticipation was one of fear rather than pleasure. "He wanted to say that he's thinking about you, thinking about you all the time."

At this the girl's face relaxed and flushed prettily.

"Thank you, sir. I asked Mr. Rogers if I could go see Will, but he won't let me."

"He is quite right," I interjected firmly. "A gaol is no place for a young girl to visit."

"I'm not put together with spit, you know," she retorted, her little chin coming up, only to drop again with a tremble to the lips as she looked toward Holmes. "If you see Will again, sir, would you tell him . . . tell him . . ."

"That you're thinking of him too?"

She nodded, blushing again. "And that . . . that I won't never give him up, no matter what anybody says. Never." With which she turned on her heel and ran off, stifling a sob as she disappeared down the hall.

We were preparing to let ourselves out when Wade Torbram called to us from the staircase. "I say, Mr. Holmes, could you spare a moment?"

He led us back into the library. Once there, however, he paused for a long moment before speaking. "This is probably not worth your while, Mr. Holmes," he eventually began, "and I have mentioned it to no one else."

"The smallest fact may be important," Holmes assured him.

The tall man gave a rueful shrug. "So I've kept telling myself. Well, here it is. During the night before the wedding, while Griffiths and I were up on the third floor, after . . . I don't know how long, I think several hours, I thought I heard a noise. Like something creaking. I looked up from the book I was reading, but the light of the lamp didn't extend much beyond the table. Griffiths said he hadn't noticed anything, though that means little as I don't think his hearing is as keen as mine. To be certain, I took the lamp and looked into the bathroom—"

"You were seated closest to it?"

"Yes, I was; Griffiths was on the other side of the table. There was nothing there, so I walked down the hall to the stairs, opened that door, and came back on the other side of the corridor."

"And again found nothing?"

"That is correct," Torbram admitted. "What is bothering me, though, is that I didn't think to look into any of those empty chambers, and now that the inspector's come up with his theory of Will's having hidden in that old lumber room... If only I'd checked! But I didn't. And, you know, one of the boards in the hall does creak."

The big man paused. "As well, I rather think I may have been on the point of dozing off and that, whatever the noise was, it was loud enough to have roused me. I can't be sure, you know, for the very nature of such a moment is that you *don't* remember it clearly. Well," he ended with a small smile, "now I've told you my great secret, and at least you haven't laughed at me."

"Far from it, Mr. Torbram," Holmes assured him, but said no more. We were soon back in the cab, which Holmes at once directed to Millbank and Horseferry Road.

"What do you think of Torbram's creaking board?" I asked.

"A valuable clue."

"Against Seeton."

"Not necessarily, for the only board in that third-floor hallway that creaks loudly is right in the middle of the corridor, half-way between the stairs and the bathroom. One would expect Seeton to have discovered it while he was laying his plans and therefore to have avoided treading on the area."

As our cab rattled across the narrow suspension

path of Lambeth Bridge, I made a small admission. "When I called on one of my patients this morning, I found her hemming barrowcoats for her coming baby. The sitting-room carpet is dark-patterned and had caught several threads from both the white flannel and the sewing."

"And what is your conclusion?"

"That there is indeed a distinct difference between thread pulled from cloth and that cut from a spool."

"Good for you, Watson. I'll yet convince you of the importance of my few inches of thread. Not to mention interest you in Lady Caroline's little toy head— her strangely ugly little toy head—and her disarranged curl papers. Perhaps even in her choice of a church for her wedding."

"Now, really, Holmes, what possible difference did that make?"

"I cannot yet say, Doctor. I merely note that the church was an unusually long way from Mowbray House and that the countess said she had no idea why it was Lady Caroline's choice. As for myself, I have been making a few discreet inquiries into the background of the wedding guests. There is not a hint that would suggest any of them should be included in our list of suspects."

"I should hope not!" I ejaculated.

"Tut, tut, Doctor, we've found a few skeletons in some rather august cupboards in our time." The cab came to a smart stop, the horse giving his head a shake that set the harness bells ringing. "Dear me, Mrs. Marshall's charity rooms rather look as if they could use a little charity themselves."

That they did. The area, banking as it does on the Thames, was of sprawling old warehouses, the invariable squashed-front public house, and those grimy small shops that pop up in every poor and crowded area. Outside a chandler's a small throng of grimy-looking customers lingered, one with some dripping tied up in a basin, another guarding the precious grains of sugar held by a conical bit of blue paper. Downright filthy barefoot children were everywhere, shouting, running, squabbling, and starting toward us.

"I ain't stayin' 'ere, gov'nor," our driver called warningly, flicking his whip at the urchin in the lead.

Holmes had already taken out a handful of small coins and now sent them flying down the road. This sent the youngsters scattering off after them, yelling like wild savages, and thus opened a brief escape for our cab. "Wait around the corner until I whistle," Holmes ordered and quickly jumped out. "Come on, Watson."

The charity rooms themselves were at the end of a long low building whose walls were too soot-darkened to retain even the vestige of any other colour; their coming fate was ominously revealed by the labels announcing that this was "Lot 4" for demolition. Across the road, boarded-up windows proclaimed GAMAGE'S TEMPORARY PREMISES, where a "Genuine Sale of Trunks and Bags" was being held; next to this THOS. BURRELL announced himself as "Dealer in Pickled Tongues, Sweetbreads, and Tripe"; the adjacent door offered the unseen premises within as "For Let"; and every blackened square yard of every building seemed to sport at least one sign blandly and ironically proclaiming the rival virtues of "Hudson" or "Sunlight Soap." Dominating the general aroma of tar and oakum was the biting reek of the Thames at low tide.

Stepping into the charity rooms we found a long space lined with trestle-tables, with innumerable boxes piled everywhere. Around the tables a dozen

---

young ladies, none of whom was Lady Caroline, with canvas aprons over their dresses, were sorting old clothing into piles. Garments of all kinds spilled over the confines of boxes and tables alike and cascaded onto the floor.

"Oh, Mrs. Marshall, do look at this!" A rosy-cheeked girl was holding up a tawdry red silk petticoat. "Just smell the awful perfume!"

"Put it in the barrel for the dustbin, my dear, for we won't give that kind of article to anyone. Could I help you, gentlemen? Why, Mr. Holmes! Whatever brings you around to us today? And Dr. Watson too."

Mrs. Marshall was exactly as I remembered her from the Blueschool Ball, a sturdy woman of some sixty years, dressed in a trim check wool bodice and skirt, with a pansy-trimmed hat pinned firmly above her curly brown fringe. From around her neck swung a gold lorgnette, the use of which had enabled her to identify us. She quickly led us into a corner away from the tables and now spoke in a lower voice. "You're here on this terrible business of the missing amethyst?"

"We are," Holmes replied, matching his tone to hers, "for we were told at Mowbray House that we would find Lady Caroline here."

Mrs. Marshall looked most surprised. "This *is* Caroline's usual day for coming in, but she hasn't been here, and most certainly we haven't expected her, not after the distressing events of last Sunday. We close in less than an hour too." An uneasy look had entered Mrs. Marshall's intelligent eyes. "Come into my office, gentlemen, where we can talk more comfortably." She turned back toward the tables and raised her voice. "Finish the boxes you've started, girls, and tidy away. Then we'll have tea."

"Yes, Mrs. Marshall" came the dutiful chorus. In

truth I think the young ladies were more than pleased to be left on their own for a few minutes, for behind us a low chatter, interspersed with many a giggle, at once broke out.

Mrs. Marshall's office was nothing more than a partitioned corner that had once, I imagine, been the shipper's quarters. The small space was now nearly filled by an old roll-top desk, and containers of garments were everywhere.

"I know you'll excuse our poor accommodation, Mr. Holmes." Mrs. Marshall pushed a crate aside in order to shut the door. "If you'll just lift that carton of boots off the chair, Dr. Watson . . . Thank you. I try to keep the best of the clothing in here, you see, for it is amazing how things have a way of disappearing the moment your back's turned, and as some recipients will make better use of what they are given than others, we try to take that into account. Now, Mr. Holmes, do tell me: is there any hope of finding poor Caroline's amethyst?"

"Inspector Macready thinks so," Holmes replied. "He has arrested the footman."

"The footman! How could the footman have taken the amethyst out of Caroline's hair in front of a whole table full of people?"

Holmes gave an outline of the inspector's theory.

"What a foolish fellow that inspector must be!" Mrs. Marshall gave a full, jolly laugh. "Is he very young?"

"Rather young, yes."

"That no doubt accounts for it. He hasn't yet had enough experience with the lower classes."

"You have much, I think."

"Forty years of charity work, Mr. Holmes, for I was my mother's assistant before I was married, and I can tell you that no lad of a footman could think up such a story-book adventure as that inspector has imagined. Hiding in empty store-rooms, and creeping into bathrooms, and picking jewel-box locks, and loosening settings, and creeping out again—all without giving himself away—and snatching the amethyst out of Caroline's back hair, and *then* swallowing it!" Again Mrs. Marshall's hearty laugh rang out. "I do hope the police won't force that young man to swallow too much castor oil, Mr. Holmes, for whatever is in him, and a longing for more pudding is apt to be the chief part, plus a liking for the second parlourmaid—"

"Mowbray House doesn't have that luxury, I'm afraid," Holmes interjected with a smile.

"Poor fellow! Then it will be dreams of the housemaid next door but one. At any rate, you can be sure he swallowed no jewels, Mr. Holmes."

"I agree with you, Mrs. Marshall."

"Do you have any idea what *did* happen to the stone?"

"I am still trying to collect data, Mrs. Marshall. Which is why," Holmes added rather pointedly, "I had hoped to see Lady Caroline here today."

Mrs. Marshall looked puzzled. "But surely you have already seen her?"

"Once, for a few minutes, on the afternoon of the wedding. Since then she has not been... available for an interview."

For a long moment there was silence, while Mrs. Marshall tapped restless fingers on her desk and stared unseeingly at an old beaver bonnet perched on the corner. "Life hasn't been easy for Caroline," she said at last. "To be born the daughter of an earl means there is so much that a girl isn't allowed to do, especially if she has a mother like the countess. Caroline is six-and-twenty, yet is treated as if she were fourteen, still being endlessly trained for the kind of marriage that depends on a large dowry and that she has therefore never had any real hope of making."

"We understand that the marriage to Mr. Stanley was the best future that could be expected for her," Holmes answered, "and that that depends on the amethyst and its sale. You have heard that Mr. Stanley left the country as soon as possible?"

Mrs. Marshall nodded, her lips tightening. "I hardly know what to think about that gentleman. On the one hand, he is quite right to guard Caroline's name, and certainly if the marriage is to be annulled, there must be no hint of cohabitation. Yet, on the other hand, his behaviour does make it so painfully clear that, in seeking the marriage, he was only interested in the five thousand pounds and not at all in Caroline."

"I really wonder if Lady Caroline will not be happier without marriage to Mr. Stanley," I said with some indignation.

Mrs. Marshall looked down at her hands, and when she finally spoke she seemed at first to have changed the subject. "Of course you don't know Lady Matilda, Lord Mowbray's sister. She too had no dowry, was never at all pretty, and had a most spineless mother. The result was that Lady Matilda has lived her whole existence in an unwanted corner of some relative's home. It wasn't even considered necessary to bring her to town for Caroline's wedding. She should have insisted, but I'm afraid Lady Matilda has used up all her stock of insistence long ago."

"And Lady Caroline?" I asked warmly. "Has she no stock of insistence still on hand?"

"I think Caroline may have more than she—or

anyone else—thinks," Mrs. Marshall replied. "I wonder where she and Mr. Mowbray have gone this morning."

"Mr. Mowbray is not with his sister," Holmes said. "At least they left Mowbray House separately."

"Oh. I see." Mrs. Marshall's frown deepened.

"Don't young ladies like shopping?" I suggested. "Perhaps the Burlington Arcade—"

"Caroline hasn't the money to buy a scarf," Mrs. Marshall replied emphatically, "nor would the countess permit her to go to the shops alone."

"The countess was lying down when Lady Caroline left. A four-wheeler was called for her, so she should be quite safe."

"Of course," Mrs. Marshall assented, but the reply was automatic; obviously her thoughts were elsewhere and her concern growing. "It is simply," she said at last, "that I cannot think of anywhere she would go."

"Lady Caroline must have found the hours since that disastrous breakfast very long," I said. "In fact, she said as much. Perhaps she has merely sought a change and is visiting a friend."

"She has none in London. I believe I might leave out the geographical qualification, for I have never heard of any residents near Mowbray Park who could possibly be so labelled. The countess has kept Caroline so circumspectly that, unable to lead the life her social position required, she has ended by having no life at all."

"You don't consider Miss Powle a friend of Lady Caroline's?" Holmes asked.

Mrs. Marshall shook a decided negative. "She is the countess's goddaughter, and the countess has never been able to do the little things for her that are usual in such a relationship. Not even having her for country visits, for no one would go willingly to Mow-bray Park. Do you know the place? Three dozen bed-rooms and not a comfortable corner anywhere. So Miss Powle was given the honour of being Caroline's attendant as a sort of payment of past obligations. I'm afraid most of the guests were chosen on much the same principle," Mrs. Marshall added, "for the wedding provided a rare opportunity for the countess to fulfil some accumulated social duties."

"How long has Lady Caroline been assisting you at these rooms, Mrs. Marshall?"

"The countess and I are family connections, Mr. Holmes, and I have long tried to make her aware of her duty to the less fortunate of this teeming city." A touch of the platform echoed through these words; I'm sure Mrs. Marshall was an impassioned speaker on the topic. "I failed so totally that she was even reluctant to permit Caroline to come. Fortunately we have young ladies from some of the highest families doing excellent work for us, and that finally con-vinced the countess that half a day a week would not do Caroline irreparable harm. For over two years, whenever she has been in town, she has come here once a week."

"Lady Caroline was willing?"

"Lady Caroline was willing to do anything," Mrs. Marshall replied grimly, "even to marry Mr. Stanley, in order to change the monotony of her life. At least," Mrs. Marshall amended thoughtfully, "she was willing to become engaged to him. I did think that, on the last few occasions I saw her before Sun-day, she was rather... *distrait.* Yes, Esther?"

A tap had come on the door, and the rosy-cheeked young girl looked in. "Excuse me, Mrs. Marshall, but there's a man asking for Lady Caroline, and I didn't know what I ought to tell him."

"A man!" Mrs. Marshall, looking startled, quickly rose. "Didn't he give his name?"

"No, he didn't."

"Some fellow from one of those dratted newspapers." Mrs. Marshall was already sallying forth, fire in her brown eyes. "One moment, Mr. Holmes, until I've sent him packing."

But Holmes was right behind her, and I at his heels. We found the dozen girls in the large room all in arrested motion, gazing with surprised expressions at the outside door. There was no man in sight.

"Where is he?" Mrs. Marshall demanded, looking around for her intended victim.

"He's . . . gone." Esther gestured her bewilderment. "All of a sudden he . . . ran away."

Holmes and I were already racing out into the street. The only man in sight was an old-clothes seller, who said that the "small gent wiv the beardeeo" had "taken h'off like a scalded cat." Since in that labyrinth of narrow passages pursuit was futile, we returned to the charity rooms to ask Esther what the visitor had been like.

"Very nice, really, most polite. A little man, very neat and clean. Grey hair," the girl added, "with a small beard."

"Was he a gentleman?" Mrs. Marshall asked shrewdly.

"Well . . ."

"Thank you, Esther. I wonder who he was," Mrs. Marshall said softly to us, her earlier frown returning.

"Not a newspaperman, you think?" I asked.

"Certainly not," Mrs. Marshall replied decisively. "No newspaperman of that age and description would be chasing around the London streets."

"I agree," Holmes said. "As I cannot think he will return, we will leave you to go on with your good work, Mrs. Marshall, and return to our own."

Outside, Holmes paused on the pavement to survey an oyster seller who had cunningly taken up a stand next to the public house, with a new "Found Drowned" announcement posted on the wall above him. With these triple attractions he was doing a brisk trade. "Did you note," Holmes asked me, "that the description of the small man with the beard is remarkably like that of my fellow night-watcher of Mowbray House?"

I had. "And," I added, "he heard Miss Esther mention your name and ran off to keep from meeting you."

"So it would seem." Holmes whistled for our cab. "Well, we can do nothing more here. Let us make another call on Sam Griffiths and see what he can tell us about that tray of lunch."

Holmes relapsing once more into an introspective mood, we exchanged not a word on the journey to Tottenham Court Road and its neighbour, Garden Row, not even when we were forced to plod along behind an omnibus, the sign on its back urging us to consume "Fry's Pure Cocoa," or when we were briefly stopped while a fire engine galloped by, the firemen shouting "Hiee—hiee—hiee!" to clear their way. The door in the end house of the terrace was opened to us by Griffiths himself, and there was no mistaking the first look in his eyes: deep consternation.

He was far too old a hand not to recover quickly, of course, and he invited us in with a good attempt at a warm welcome. He fussed with the fire, the chairs, the cushions, and, explaining that his wife was out, offered a "drop" to keep out the cold.

Holmes was a sharper file than he, however, and waited him out with the most bland courtesy. At last Griffiths had to seat himself, and, as Holmes said that he found the fire too warm and at the last moment adroitly transferred himself into the chair that Griffiths had been about to take, our host had to sit where the light from the gas lamp on the wall fell full on his perspiring face.

"What can I do for you gentlemen?" he inquired, with a forced heartiness that could not disguise the changes that had come over him. The plump face was now flaccid and the blooming colour reduced to mottled patches.

"Take us over the same old ground, I'm afraid," Holmes replied lightly. "A boring necessity of investigations, Mr. Griffiths, as you'll know."

"Bless you, sir, *I* know all about it." Though his reply was both prompt and firm, moisture was collecting on his brow.

"I haven't yet made much progress," Holmes went on. "Perhaps you've heard of Inspector Macready's belief that the footman is the thief?"

Griffiths nodded. "I've heard of it, sir, and between us three, it's nonsense. Flat-out nonsense. Nobody could 'ave crept along that there 'all, and into the bathroom and back out again, and off downstairs, without Mr. Torbram or me seeing or 'earing 'im." This was said heartily, too heartily.

"You were the one facing the back stairs, I understand."

"I was, sir," Griffiths replied stoutly. Beads of sweat were now standing on his face.

"And you neither saw nor heard anything at all?"

"I did not, sir. As I said, *nothing.*" Again there was too much emphasis to carry conviction.

"How about Mr. Torbram?" Holmes persisted. "Did he hear or see anything?"

"'E did once think 'e'd 'eard something like a board creaking. Or so 'e said, and got up and walked all around. 'E didn't find nothing, and that didn't surprise me."

"I understand that you had a tray of lunch left ready for you to take upstairs."

"We did, sir, thanks to the cook's kindness." This was said quite naturally. Whatever the cause of Griffith's unease, I didn't think the lunch was worrying him.

"Mrs. Grogan suggested it, did she?"

"I can't rightly say about that, sir. She got it ready, that I know, and set it on the back-stairs landing. When Mr. Torbram and I went on duty, I carried the tray up and set it on the table, and a very comforting thing it was to see as we sat there, I assure you." In spite of his breezy words, a trickle of sweat had started down his face, and he wiped it away with a furtive hand.

"What was on the tray?"

Griffith's description, though more detailed, fitted Seeton's.

"When did you have the lunch?" Holmes persisted.

"The first bit about two, sir. Mr. Torbram 'ad been reading most of the time up to then, and 'e looked up and said 'e was near froze and 'ow about 'aving a bite. I was more than willing, so Mr. Torbram lighted the spirit burner to 'eat the coffee up, and we set to. Very welcome it was."

"You didn't finish all the coffee and the food then?"

Griffiths shook his head. "There was more than we needed for the one go, like, so we left near 'alf.

Then later Mr. Torbram said he felt near ready to drop, and I felt *I'd* be better for a wake-up cup—"

Holmes swiftly interrupted. "Why was that?"

"Well, you know what it's like on a long watch, sir," the man replied, and, bringing out his handkerchief, wiped his face so that he was fairly hidden behind the cloth. But he had at length to emerge, and Holmes was waiting for him. Ever more assertive questions and ever more evasive answers followed until finally, with tears starting in his bleary eyes, Griffiths conceded the truth.

"It's a thing that's never 'appened to me before—never, sir—not in all my years on the force, nor since. It must 'ave been the sitting still that did it, for usually a chap can move around 'ow 'e likes on such a job. But Mr. Torbram was afraid of disturbing the family down below us, so by and large we just sat. That's what must 'ave done it, sir, that's all I can say."

"Done what?" Holmes insisted, though the answer was clear enough.

"Made me doze off, sir," Griffiths said miserably. "I come to, my 'ead on my chest, to find Mr. Torbram staring off down the 'all. 'What was that?' 'e was asking. Well, I 'ad to say I'd never 'eard nothing, and God knows *that* was the truth. But whether I would 'ave if I'd been as alert as I should 'ave been . . . When Mr. Torbram didn't find nothing, I didn't figure as 'ow my little lapse 'ad done any 'arm, and I don't think Mr. Torbram 'ad even noticed it. Leastwise, 'e said nothing.

"Even the other evening when you told me about the amethyst 'aving been stole, I thought all the wrong doings 'ad 'appened the next morning, so the events of the night, like, didn't matter. But since then I've 'eard from some of my old mates, and they told me about the inspector and 'is idea, and I 'aven't 'ad a moment's peace since." Certainly the man looked utterly wretched now.

"When did your little nap occur?"

"All I can say, sir, is it was sometime after two, when we 'ad our first lunch, and nigh on four-thirty when Mr. Torbram asked me if I'd 'eard anything."

"After that you had your second lunch. Did that seem to wake you up?"

"It did, sir, though I won't say but what I felt 'eavy-'eaded, like, the rest of the night. From the cold, I expect." Griffiths took a long breath. "I know I should 'ave told all this to the inspector, sir, I know it well. But I just couldn't bring myself to do it. After all my years, with never a blot on my name, and now, at my time of life, and with the nice bit extra I been making with these guard jobs—"

Holmes broke into this woeful recitation. "I really don't think you can be blamed, Mr. Griffiths, nor do I see any reason to inform the inspector."

Griffiths' face lighted up wonderfully, though he stoutly said, "If you think it's my duty, sir, I will."

"If he asks, no doubt you should tell him," Holmes replied carefully, and, refusing to say more, led the way out.

As we started back toward Tottenham Court Road I said positively, "Holmes, something in that lunch was drugged."

"I agree. Probably in the cups, for the first drink produced slumber, the second did not. With only one small lamp for light, a few drops of liquid at the bottom of a cup would be unlikely to be noticed."

"With that tray left on the lower floor landing, any-one in the house could have had access to it."

"I agree once more."

"Torbram said that he thought he was on the point

125

of dozing," I recalled. "Perhaps he was farther into sleep than he thinks, or of course the drug may not have affected him as much. The whole episode, though, surely bolsters the inspector's case against Seeton, for his risk would have been much less if he knew the watchers would be drugged. If he was listening nearby, he would hear the little clatter of the lunch consumption and then everything fall quiet."

"Quite so," Holmes replied, "yet none of this is an answer for the kind of damage that has been done to the setting of the clip, and that is the most major problem to the solution of the case."

I had momentarily forgotten this and could still think of no explanation. "You have also pointed out," I counted the items on my fingers, "the scratched bark on the plane tree, the bit of thread on the bathroom floor, the lad in the check trousers—"

"The very clumsy lad in the check trousers."

"Well, yes, though I can't see that that makes any difference." Holmes made no answer, and I continued my enumerating. "Then there are Lady Caroline's loosened hair papers, the little toy head she had in her pocket, and her choice of a church for her wedding." I paused; Holmes still said nothing. "That is," I added, "if you consider these details of any importance." When Holmes gave no response, I asked challengingly, "*Can* you think of any explanation?"

"To a good number of them I can," Holmes replied, with obvious dissatisfaction, "though the theory is not one that I am yet ready to share. At the moment it suffers from a plethora of surmise, and therefore is all too much like the inspector's hypothesis."

We had reached Tottenham Court Road, and a cab was coming toward us. As I hailed it, Holmes said, almost as if he were speaking only to himself,

"Those old books in Lord Mowbray's library: why should they have been mutilated?"

"Probably that has no connection with the case."

"Perhaps. Yet when oddities cluster around one central fact, as they are beginning to do here..." Holmes said no more, not even to answer my farewell when he left the cab at Baker Street.

Chapter VII

Some must watch
—Shakespeare, *Hamlet,*
act 3, sc. 2, line 289

I had hardly undressed for bed that evening when our doorbell was frantically rung. During the day the cold weather had continued to moderate, and toward night rain had started. The result was that a carriage had overturned on the wet cobbles of Mortimer Street; as Anstruther was not at home, I had to go. I found the coachman unconscious, the footman trapped with one leg underneath, and a mother with a broken arm more worried about the slight cut on her daughter's pretty forehead.

When I was at last able to return home, the rain had ceased, the clouds were breaking, and the late dawn of a winter's day was touching the skies with opal. I checked my watch and groaned to find it already after eight o'clock. Abandoning all thoughts of sleep in favour of a quick bath and a hearty breakfast, I started on my day's calls. By a little judicial arranging, I was able to move steadily in the direction of Baker Street. I was leaving my last patient, on Edgeware Road, when a familiar strident voice hailed me from a hansom.

"If not at Philippi, Doctor, then sufficiently near it and most certainly well met. I was heading for Paddington, hoping to find you free for an hour. You are on your rounds?"

"I'm free for the day," I replied, climbing into the cab with conscious virtue. "Where are we headed?"

"Once more to Mowbray House. I hope soon to convince Lady Caroline that my patience will outlast her determination."

"You think she is purposefully avoiding you?"

"I think that has become so obvious that the only question is why."

"What of last night? Did your Irregulars track your fellow watcher to his lair?"

"He never appeared, and neither did Eustace leave the house. Most annoying."

"Has Wiggins as yet learned anything of that young fellow in the check trousers?"

"Nothing, though as we really have little idea of where or when to look, that is probably not surprising. What Wiggins has reported are some developments on the Fitzgerald front. Our Irishman has transferred to the respectable confines of the Traveller's, no doubt because he is now being dogged at a discreet distance by a little chap with ginger whiskers and a much-worn air of gentility."

"A bookmaker's tout."

"Worse. Bengie Daniels is a former bailiff and later convict and now the best spy of the underworld. He's an expensive limpet, though, and that suggests that Fitzgerald's shady creditors have banded together. They're no doubt afraid that, should his uncle die and Fitzgerald inherit, he'll slip off overseas again, leaving his lawyers to handle his recognized debts and everyone else out in the financial cold."

"I can't see what they hope to gain by following Fitzgerald about," I objected. "Even if he should inherit a fortune, he won't carry it in his pockets."

"I suspect Bengie's pockets contain a paper which, once Fitzgerald's signature is on it, would become legal tender."

"Then I suppose this Bengie has some rough friends within call?"

"You suppose correctly. My brother Mycroft, whose rooms you'll remember are close to the Traveller's, reports a whole cohort of them, uneasy at being in the unfamiliar territory of Pall Mall, but manfully remaining within whistle range of Bengie even so."

"Does Fitzgerald know he's being followed?"

"He's much too experienced not to, and his move to the Traveller's was most surely made to cramp Bengie's style."

Here we pulled up at Mowbray House, and had the door opened to us by Rogers. One look at his martyred expression told us that fresh troubles had descended. As we stepped into the hall, we could see that the seals on the dining-room door had been broken, and from within came a miscellany of busy noises.

Holmes cocked his head quizzically. "Has Lord Mowbray decided to move his household to the country, lock, stock, and barrel?"

"It's the police, sir, half a dozen of them. And half a dozen convicts," the harassed butler added, "couldn't be more destructive of the order of a place."

"Dear me! What has caused this new invasion?"

"They are looking," Rogers replied from between nearly clenched teeth, "for Lady Caroline's amethyst, sir."

"I was under the impression that they had already looked for Lady Caroline's amethyst."

"So was I, sir."

"Does this mean that even the might of castor oil has failed to produce the stone?" Holmes asked, his mouth twitching.

Rogers was far from finding anything amusing in the situation. "Will hasn't been released, sir, that's all I know. That and the fact that it's near impossible to run a household in such a situation as this. You never know what's happening from one hour to another, whether it'll be luncheon served in the back parlour in a civilized manner, or trays in the bedchambers. And the women downstairs that upset, and what comfort can I offer? I tell them it's all in God's hands, but what help is that to Mrs. Grogan when she doesn't know whether to roast a rack of lamb or order in a ham for more sandwiches? Surely this isn't going to go on much longer, sir?"

"I hope not, Rogers. We will at least try to make our own visit as short as possible. Would Lady Caroline be able to see us for a few moments?"

"Lady Caroline has gone down to Mowbray Park, sir." I, who knew Holmes so well, sensed the surprise that stiffened his figure. "Mr. Eustace went with her on the train early last evening. Lady Caroline said that she wanted to get away from all the worry here, and I'm sure you can't wonder, sir."

"Has the inspector been persistent with his questioning of the poor young lady?"

"I can't say that he has, sir," Rogers made the concession grudgingly, "only that once on the day of the wedding, and no doubt that was necessary."

"The newspapers have probably been rather trying," Holmes suggested.

"They would have, sir, if I'd permitted their impertinence," Rogers replied loftily. "I made the women understand that they were to remain completely indoors as long as this . . . this situation lasted. *I* have seen to all errands, and *I* have answered all doors. So the press very soon left Mowbray House alone."

"Very wise. How long is Lady Caroline to remain in the country?"

"I couldn't say, sir. She may well not return to London. I know his lordship wants to move the household back to Mowbray Park as soon as possible."

"Let us hope that he will soon be able to do so," Holmes said soothingly. "Now if I could trouble you to call Essie again for a few moments?"

"Certainly, sir." Rogers led the way to the library. "This room was the first searched by the police this morning. I begged that favour of the inspector" (this said with heavy sarcasm) "so that there would be at least one corner where a visitor could be shown and left in peace." With which the butler stalked off.

He had no sooner gone than from across the hall came a loud crash, blended with loud expostulations of *"Will* you watch what you're doing there!" and "Clumsy fool!"

"Come, Watson." Holmes, who had again been peering at the few books still on the library shelves, darted for the door. "I can't resist this."

We found a scene that resembled preparations for a furniture sale. Two plainclothesmen had taken out all the drawers of a serpentine chest, in the process dropping one of them; a jumble of writing paper, pens, old cuff-links, a pencil or two, and other such small goods were now spread over the carpet, threatening to interfere with the work of two more men. They had turned back the edge of the carpet for a good foot along one side and were closely inspecting every inch of this strip. Inspector Macready was at the side of the room, sombrely contemplating the broad derrière of yet another officer, on his hands and knees at the hem of the window draperies.

"And who's been eating *my* porridge?" Holmes inquired. "Good afternoon, Inspector. You seem to be having a game of three bears, or is it 'Button, button, who's got the button?'"

The young inspector was unusually pale, and his boisterous manner had been replaced by a belligerent defensiveness. His gaze was close to a glare, and his tone brusque. "Seeton didn't swallow the amethyst. He couldn't have got far, though, so we'll find it." A metallic clatter came from below our feet, as if half a dozen saucepans had been dropped, and a woman's voice rose in loud complaint. "We're also working downstairs," Macready unnecessarily added.

"You don't think it possible, just possible," Holmes asked softly, "that Seeton isn't the thief?"

This brought back the fire to the inspector's drawn face. "No, I do not," he retorted loudly. Holmes turned on his heel and walked out, and I followed him. You can do little to help a man with a mind as closed as the inspector's.

We found Essie waiting for us in the library, and she at once began the litany of her distress. "Oh, sir, *can't* you do something for my poor Will? He's still in gaol, and he's as innocent as I am."

"Where is the proof of that, Essie?" Holmes asked, giving his head a dubious shake.

"Oh, sir, don't say *you* think he's guilty!"

"I have as yet no positive proof of his innocence."

"If you did, sir, could you get Will free?"

"Certainly I am helpless to do so as matters stand." The girl's pale face was full of longing, though she said not a word. "Come, Essie, why are you so sure yourself? Aren't you perhaps indulging in some wishful thinking?"

"Not about my Will's innocence I'm not, sir. I know that as well's I know anything."

Holmes said nothing, only kept his sympathetic eyes steadily on her. Nearly distraught as she was, the poor girl was soon in tears and, between sobs, finally poured out her secret. She knew that Will hadn't been hiding on the top floor on the night before the wedding because . . . he had been in her room.

I would have issued a warning as to the dangers of such behavior; Holmes continued with his calm questioning. "I see. Your room is on the second floor, isn't it?"

"Yes, sir, at the back." She wiped her eyes and fought to control her sobs. "Will's is downstairs, next to Mr. Rogers', so of course we couldn't go there. The rooms on both sides of me are empty, and there's only Mr. Eustace on the corner, and he—" She broke off abruptly, the flush from her tears rapidly turning to pallor.

"What about Mr. Eustace?"

For some minutes Essie remained dumb, her handkerchief pressed to her mouth, renewed sobs shaking her shoulders. Holmes had repeatedly to assure her that her information would be used only for the possible recovery of the amethyst and the freeing of Will before she would say another word. Then at last we had the whole, all-too-human, little story.

As we had already been told, Essie was the daughter of the old Mowbray Park coachman, and so had gone into service at a very young age. While she liked her work well enough and was proud of her rise to the position of lady's maid, she had been very lonely among the dozen elderly servants who made up the rest of the Mowbray staff. Will's arrival was thus a great event to her, and he, also suffering from the twin loss of family and friends, reciprocated her interest. The ample opportunities offered by the unused rooms and unkempt gardens of Mowbray Park had done the rest.

Once the household had moved to London, however, all was perforce changed. Will and Essie were both kept busy from morning to night, and were forbidden by the cautious Rogers to take their half-days together. After some weeks of mutual unsatisfied longing, the night finally came when the desperate Will had crept up to Essie's room and been warmly received. They had thought they were as quiet as mice, but when Will had at last tiptoed out into the corridor, the aghast pair found Eustace lounging there.

He had at once ushered them back into Essie's room and shut the door. *He* had no objection to their having a bit of fun, he had reassuringly whispered, but the triple hierarchy of his parents and Rogers was another matter. If they ever found out, dismissal for both young lovers, with no character and hence a dismal future, was certain. They needn't worry, though, Eustace had gone on to his stricken audience, for the price of his permanent silence was simple: he wanted a front-door key, and Will valeted his father. Couldn't Will manage to borrow the key long enough to have a copy made?

At this the young footman had suddenly grinned, and said that he didn't need to borrow the key for a little job like that: a bit of wax was all that was needed. To Eustace's frank admiration, the day after his next afternoon off, Will had produced a new front-door key. Thereafter Eustace was out for several hours nearly every night, and whether out or in paid no attention to the happenings in the room down the hall.

"Can you tell me exactly when Mr. Eustace received his key, Essie?" Holmes asked.

"Right after the Lord Mayor's show, sir. Will wanted to take me, but Mr. Rogers wouldn't give me the half-day off, so he took his mother and little sister. He brought me back ever such a brave set of ribbons."

"And picked up the key from a certain little house off Portobello Road, I fancy."

"I don't know anything about that, sir. All Will ever said was there's aplenty 'round his old home natty enough to do the job. I've been thinking and thinking," Essie went on with some fresh tears, "what to do. If I tell, me and Will'll be out on our ear sure's breathing, and for what? Likely nobody'll believe me. They'll say I'm just lying to save Will."

"Wouldn't Mr. Eustace be believed?" I asked.

"He hasn't spoke up yet, sir, has he? And you can't blame him all that much. He'd get it pretty hot for keeping quiet so long, and he can't explain about the latchkey, can he?"

"I think you would be wise to keep silent for at least a while longer," Holmes said. "Have you ever seen Will in a pair of loud check trousers?"

"No." Essie looked genuinely surprised. "Never, sir. Will's right choice over his clothes; if he's any old things like that at home, he'd leave 'em there for his young brother. My Will's no jipe, sir."

"We'll hope all ends well with him. I understand that Lady Caroline has gone to Mowbray Park."

"She has that, sir, on the early train last evening. Her and Mr. Eustace."

"Mr. Eustace will return here?"

Essie shook her head. "Not that he don't want to, for he hates the country like poison, but his lordship said that, once Mr. Eustace got to Mowbray Park, he was to stay put. That is, unless something happens about the amethyst to bring Lady Caroline back, and I don't think she's expecting that, poor lady. She was crying when she got home from those charity rooms yesterday, and that's something she hasn't done afore, not even on that awful wedding day."

"Did something happen at the charity rooms to upset Lady Caroline afresh?" Holmes asked, with some duplicity since we well knew that she had never gone there.

"She never said, sir, but myself I think it was just being with the other young ladies and knowing, innardly, that she wasn't unmarried like most of them, yet she hadn't got her husband waiting at home for her neither."

"We'll be seeing Will when we leave here," Holmes said. "Would you write him a note to tell him that you've confided your secret to us, and that he should tell us everything also?"

Essie accepted Holmes's notebook without a demure and, perching on the chair by the desk, scribbled a few words. I must have been looking as disapproving as I felt all through Essie's recital, for as she rose she suddenly gazed full into my face. "I'm not going to give Will up, not if I have to wait 'til I'm fruz solid," she said defiantly and ran out.

"Do you believe the girl's account, Holmes?" I asked as we gathered up our hats and gloves.

"Certainly if Will has begun spending his nights in Essie's arms, it would explain why Rogers has found him increasingly inattentive at his duties." Holmes opened the library door and paused. "What have we here?"

In the hall Wade Torbram was standing by the stairs, watching a stout policeman mount a step-ladder that had been placed under the portrait of the third earl. As we stepped into the hall, the secretary was asking in awestruck tones, "Are you going to search every inch of Mowbray House?"

"Not of the whole place, sir," the policeman replied, "for it's not likely that there footman could've got as far as upstairs, say, without somebody noticing 'e wasn't where 'e was supposed to be."

"Surely he couldn't have absented himself for even a few seconds without being missed," I objected, "not on a morning as busy as that must have been."

"It don't seem likely, sir, that I'll grant you." The policeman had lifted the picture down and, resting it on the top of the step-ladder, was subjecting the frame to close scrutiny. "The trouble is everybody is willing to swear 'e didn't disappear for *more* than a few seconds, but nobody is willing to swear 'e didn't make himself scarce at *all*. Not even that there butler, and who knows 'ow far we can trust 'im anyways?" He rehung the picture and climbed heavily down. "That there 'earth," he asked, looking toward the opposite wall, "was there a fire in it that morning?"

Torbram shook his head. "Just in the dining-room."

The policeman sighed. "So 'ere's another place that'll 'ave to be searched, and a nice dirty job that'll be too."

"I don't wish to add to your labours," Torbram said slowly, "but, do you know, I don't think fire would destroy amethyst. Would it, Mr. Holmes?"

"Certainly not the heat in the outer part of such ordinary hearths as these."

The policeman's eyes widened. "Lor' love a duck!

That there 'earth in the dining-room 'as been swept out and all. Who'd 'ave the doing of that, now?"

"Well," Torbram hesitated, "if he'd been here, Will."

"And since 'e 'asn't been 'ere, being otherwise h'occupied at the station-'ouse?"

"Rogers."

"You saw 'im at it?"

"Yes."

"*In*deed." The policeman was already heading for the dining-room. "I think I'll just 'ave a word with the inspector."

"Oh dear!" With a wry smile Torbram watched him go. "I'm glad I didn't tell *him* anything about that creaking floor-board."

"Quite," Holmes agreed.

But he said no more, and Torbram trailed after us down the hall. At the front door he said hesitantly, "I don't suppose you have been able to . . ."

"I have not got as far as I had hoped to do in this time," Holmes replied, "but I am getting closer to a solution."

"Are you?" I asked eagerly, as soon as we were alone outside.

"I think so." Again, he said no more, only showed me what Essie had written in his notebook: "Dear Will. Tell Mr. Holmes about us like I have. Always thinking of you. Your Essie."

When we reached the station-house, these few words completed the change in Will's demeanor toward us. With his head up and eyes steady, he confirmed Essie's story in all particulars.

"Why don't you marry the girl?" I interjected sternly, unable to keep quiet any longer.

"'Ow can we, sir?" Will protested. "We'd lose our places right off, and what would we do then?"

139

"What happens when Essie gets in the family way?"

"She ain't goin' to get in no fambly way," Will retorted. "Us knows a few things, us does. Leastwise," he added, "*I* does. Yer don't come from Nottin' 'Ill way and be such a muff as that."

"You also know how to make a wax press," Holmes observed, "and who will cut a key from it."

"'Course I do," Will retorted. "So's my little brother, and 'e's not ten yet. Look, sir, it's like this. What I did, I did for me and Essie, but I ain't sayin' I didn't feel sorry for Mr. Eustace too. The age of 'im, and son of an earl and all, and not 'lowed yer own latchkey! *I* don't blame 'im for what 'e did, and I don't think what me and Essie did's so wrong neither. Us ain't blocks of wood wiv no feelin's, for all us're in service."

At that point we left and walked along Waterloo Road watching for a cab. We had nearly reached the bridge when Holmes spoke. "You said you had finished your medical duties for the day, Doctor. Could you spare the time to go down to Mowbray Park?"

"To see Lady Caroline? Or Eustace?"

"Both, if you can. Far more important is simply to ascertain that they are indeed there."

"Where else could they be?" I asked, surprised. "They have obviously gone with the knowledge and approval of their parents, and where else would they permit Lady Caroline to go? A girl who has so few friends that she had none at her wedding?"

"I know, Watson, I know, and yet *why* has she gone? She has *not* been badgered by either the police or the newspapers, and while her life in Mowbray House is dismal enough, can you believe she will be much better off at the family place in Kent, which will now even be without the skilled services of such as Rogers and the cook? I would go down myself except that you have a better chance of being successful: Lady Caroline would surely once again find some excuse not to see me."

"You cannot be sure of that, Holmes," I protested, though without conviction.

"From what except the fear of my questions has she fled?"

For that I had no answer. For a long moment Holmes stayed motionless, staring unseeingly at the road by his feet. A drayman had pulled up across from us and was having a mug of hot tea from a barrow, while his horse munched contentedly from his nosebag. Around the animal's feet half a dozen pigeons hopped busily, picking up the stray grains that dropped onto the setts. Slowly Holmes roused, and, pointing at the birds with his stick, observed, "That is what I am doing, picking up a fact here and there and hoping ultimately to fill my crop. So if you could make a short visit to Mowbray Park, I would be much obliged. There is a train from Charing Cross within the hour, and one back later this evening."

I made some quick calculations. "I can send a note to Mary and Anstruther. Yes, I could manage the trip."

"My most hearty thanks, Doctor."

From Charing Cross I dispatched a special messenger to my wife and to my helpful medical neighbour. As I climbed onto the train, Holmes said, "If Lady Caroline is at Mowbray Park, all is well. Until tomorrow, Watson."

If Lady Caroline is at Mowbray Park, all is well.

These words kept repeating in my mind as I crossed the Downs and the miles clicked by.

———

• • •

When I stepped off the train onto the short High Street of Mowbray village, my gaze was involuntarily jerked up to a frowning grey stone tower that seemed to stand no more than yards away and to loom like a heavy shadow over the dozen small buildings that were clustered at its feet. This I had not expected, and feeling rather stunned, I stood for a moment staring up at the threatening solidity, broken only by narrow slits of openings and very few of these.

"Takes a bit of getting used to, don't it, sir?" The station-master had come up behind me. "Fair looks ready to gobble you up—aye, and to keep you forever too. Never been 'ere before, 'ave you, sir?"

I agreed, adding the prevarication that I had a small delivery to make to Lady Caroline.

The station-master's eyes widened. "Bless you, sir, someone's given you wrong directions. The young lady's in London. At least," he amended, "she might be away now, I don't rightly know about that, but she's married a City gent and will be living in London from now on. No, no, sir, Mr. Eustace ain't 'ere neither, nor more is 'is lordship nor the countess. They've all been gone for weeks."

"I must have misunderstood," I said, trying to keep from showing how startled I was.

"You ain't the only one neither," the station-master said, "for a chap came on the train last evening, a little fellow with one of those pointed beards, who was under the same mistook. Got off the train 'e did and stood looking around, 'is 'at in 'is 'and, if you'll believe me, as if 'e was expecting somebody else to get off. Of course nobody did—there's 'ardly ever anybody for Mowbray. Finally 'e asks me if nobody 'ad come. I told 'im no. 'Not Lady Caroline Mowbray?' 'e says, with a gasp. 'Nor Mr. Eustace Mowbray?' I told 'im no again.

"But 'e wouldn't be said, and off 'e marched 'imself up to Mowbray Park and talked to Mrs. 'Ardy, the 'ousekeeper. Of course she told 'im the same, it being the truth, so back 'e 'ad to come, looking most put about. Asked if there wasn't no train back to London last night. Some nights there is, some there isn't, and last night was one of the second kind. 'Best thing you can do,' I told 'im, 'is to cross over to the Mowbray Arms and see if they can put you up. They don't get much trade nowadays,' I said, 'but I dare say they'd manage something. Then you can take the train back to London in the morning,' I said. And that's what 'e done, 'aving Hobson's choice in the matter.

"See Mowbray Park yourself, sir? You might as well, there not being a train back to London for a couple of hours. Just go around the corner there and on up the 'ill. Send a telegram? Just you write it out, sir, and it'll be sent."

My message to Holmes was brief, merely telling him that neither Lady Caroline nor Eustace had arrived at their country home, and that a man who resembled his fellow watcher had come down yesterday evening looking for them and had returned to London by the morning train.

I then walked to the end of the High Street and turned left up the hill that began the short steep ascent to Mowbray Park.

The building was of the same century as the town house, with the turreted remains of the donjon that so severely guarded the little village older still. All around me were what had no doubt once been noble grounds. As I passed by the deserted post house and pushed my way through the yawning gates, I could see to my right a sprawling wooded area well dotted with the stumps of sacrificed giants, and to the left a wilderness of tangled shrubbery that led to the leaf-filled depression of the old moat. Broken statuary lined the roadway, and the very gravel beneath my feet had been so trodden down through the years that it was traversed by deep frozen ruts of mud.

The house itself was, from a distance, magnificent, a central block of yellow stone, and two wings of half-timber. But the ring of the bell was thin and distant, the wait for it to be answered very long, and the servant who finally appeared an elderly woman in a worn stuff dress and limp apron, who blinked up at me in very dim comprehension.

I played out the necessary charade by asking for Lord Mowbray, and was of course told that he was in London. I then asked for the countess and was naturally told the same. At that I asked for the housekeeper.

I was led into the huge entrance room and left, perched on a black wicker settee that surely belonged in a garden, contemplating a dismal array of stuffed animal heads whose glassy yellow eyes seemed to accuse me of having something to do with their present predicament.

The old housekeeper was a tiny body in black bombazine and fearsome cap, who assured me that all the family was in London. "For Lady Caroline's wedding, you see, sir. She was married last Sunday." This was said with all the pride of a long-time servant: apparently not a hint of the trouble that had fallen upon the poor young lady had as yet reached her old home. "Would you like to see the Great Hall, sir?"

This was so obviously expected that I agreed and was taken to the end of the entrance room and through huge doors whose blackened wood still retained the marks of the mighty axe that had shaped them.

A Great Hall it most certainly was, wrapped in a gloom that felt as if it had been undisturbed for centuries. My first glance found no furnishings of any kind, and my eyes were drawn up and still up, where forty feet above our heads stretched a hammer-beam roof, its bosses carved with scroll-bearing angels. High in the walls fine oriel windows glowed in the last rays of the setting sun, and ahead stretched from one side to the other a mighty hearth, vaulted in dull red stone.

"Magnificent," I said truthfully and was interrupted by a faint rhythmic tinkle somewhere near my left elbow. Peering into the deep shadows, I found a gilt-bedecked mantel clock perched incongruously on a mahogany games table; with apologetic and metallic notes, it said that it was now five o'clock.

"That dates from the last century, sir," the old housekeeper said proudly, "and belonged to the eldest daughter of the ninth earl."

"Indeed," I said, thinking it a safe observation.

A majestic three-quarter chime came from behind me. A carriage clock, perched at the end of a Chinese lacquered chest. Next to it was an ormolu contraption flanked by enameled caryatides and crowned with floral garlands, and saying on its dial that it was nearly four-thirty.

"Why," I asked in bewilderment, "are these clocks here, all by themselves like this?"

"Well," the housekeeper paused as if the question were new to her, "they aren't anywhere else, sir."

145

An answer fit for a philosopher!

I thanked Mrs. Hardy, offered half a crown, which was refused with a curtsy, and left.

In the village I had a glass of porter at the Mowbray Arms. That a second stranger from London should have an interest in the first seemed a natural conclusion to the host and his few customers, and I had no difficulty in collecting innumerable details about the stranger. If a description of his ring, which was of dull gold that yet looked "right rich," would help Holmes identify him, or yet his preference for oatmeal porridge over a nice fry, I had notes enough to satisfy even his appetite for facts.

I dozed steadily on the way back to London, but my sleep was uneasy, and I think I arrived more tired than if I had stayed awake. I felt bound to put my notes at Holmes's disposal as soon as possible and, assuming that he would be again on guard at Mowbray House, directed my cab there. As soon as we rounded the Archbishop's Park I instructed the driver to proceed at a walking pace, but I had not a glimpse of anyone, much less of either Holmes or the little man who was nearly, though not quite, a gentleman. Mowbray House itself was in pitch-darkness, and I had perforce to direct the cab on to Baker Street. The house there too appeared wrapped in deep slumber, so I contented myself with scribbling a few words on the back of my pages of notes and pushing these under the door.

As I at last headed home, I felt that my trip to the country had at least answered one question: the watcher of Mowbray House was trying to see Lady Caroline. The important questions now were why, who was he, and where was the young lady?

I tried to feel secure in the high probability that her brother was with her, but remembering all too well the elegant ineffectuality of Eustace, I went to my bed very uneasy.

Mary was waiting up for me, and I at once confided my concerns to her. She was not reassuring. "Wherever can she be?" was her instant exclamation.

For us, anxiety over Lady Caroline's fate had completely submerged our earlier curiosity over the disappearance of her amethyst.

Chapter VIII

Man is the hunter
—Alfred, Lord Tennyson,
The Princess, part 5, line 147

I had intended catching a few hours of sleep before starting my medical rounds, and my note to Holmes had accordingly concluded with the hope of seeing him early on the following afternoon. Morpheus, however, is a most unreliable god; it was late when I finally slept, much later when I woke. I dragged myself off to start the day, sending another note to Holmes to say that I would call when I could. It was nearly four when I at last heavily mounted the seventeen steps to our old rooms.

I must have looked as exhausted as I felt, for Holmes's greeting was "Did you have any lunch, Watson? Nor I, for I have just climbed from bed myself. A high tea is surely in order." And he rang the bell for Mrs. Hudson.

"You were at Mowbray House again last night?" I asked, settling into my old chair with a weary sigh. "I drove by and didn't see you."

"I was *incognito* as a guinea sack next to a dustbin." Here Mrs. Hudson entered, and Holmes paused to give her our order. "Your passing cab was the only event of my vigil," he went on. "That my fellow watcher did not appear was of course to be expected after your interesting discoveries at Mowbray Park. Well done, Watson."

Words of even this modest praise were infrequent enough from Holmes for me to feel a satisfaction that amply repaid me for my efforts.

"There can now be little doubt," Holmes continued, leaning back in his chair and fitting his fingertips together with nice precision, "that the small man with the goatee has been watching Mowbray House because of Lady Caroline, and that, up to the day before yesterday at least, he knew no more of her whereabouts than we do. After returning here and finding your note, I spent the remaining hours of the night conversing with cabmen, trying to find one who had picked up the mystery man at Charing Cross yesterday morning. The task would have been impossible without our quarry's facial appendage; looking like a 'foreign gent' made him memorable enough for his driver to recall him."

"I wonder how he learned of Lady Caroline's supposed return to Kent."

"I wondered that myself and decided to ask Rogers for a few details. He told me that, when he had whistled for a cab for Lady Caroline and Eustace, as it pulled up at Mowbray House a little man with a beard, who seemed to have been passing by, lingered quite close to the cab. Rogers, ever the courteous servant, responded to the stranger's well-dressed appearance by asking if he could be of assistance. The little man asked if Rogers would whistle for a cab for him, and Rogers did so. Unfortunately for the stranger, there was no response for several minutes, so no doubt by the time he reached Charing Cross he had to scramble quickly onto the train, and thus went down to Mowbray Park unaware that neither Lady Caroline nor Eustace was aboard. Could you make a guess as to his identity?"

At this point Mrs. Hudson re-entered, bearing a well-laden tray. As soon as she had left, even as Holmes poured our tea, I asked, "Do you mean I know this little man who has been tracking Lady Caroline?"

"You know of him, as do I: Arthur Manning, the expert gemmologist of Gerrard's."

"Good Lord!" I stopped in the process of dropping sugar into my cup and stared in amazement. "The man who appraised the Thistle clip for the marriage negotiations, who took it to Mowbray House—"

"And who was so deeply upset when he learned of the stone's disappearance that he nearly fainted. More, he wished to see Lady Caroline then, if you remember, ostensibly to express his sympathy."

"Rather a forward desire for a mere jeweller," I observed, taking two of Mrs. Hudson's superb potted-meat sandwiches.

"Most certainly he hasn't been haunting Mowbray House on these past frigid nights, nor going to those miserable charity rooms, nor yet down to Kent, merely in order to express his sympathy. I have discovered another interesting fact about Mr. Manning: he collects gems."

"He can afford to buy them?"

"He is certainly a highly valued employee of Gerrard's, and as well his criteria for his collection is apparently historic association with royalty rather than high quality of the stones. He is known to have bought a pearl ring owned by Elizabeth of Bohemia, a miniature of the Duchess of Albany framed in chips of diamonds, a garnet brooch that belonged to some Polish princess, and a mere coral necklace that had been used to ease the toothing pains of one of the Dukes of Grafton."

"Nothing of great value in that collection," I agreed.

"Manning is also believed to have recently bought a sapphire bracelet in which the stone is badly flawed—the bracelet was once the property of Aubrey de Vere's daughter—while at the same sale turning down an exquisite necklace that was being offered at a bargain price."

"The necklace has no royal connection?"

"None. Fresh from Fabergé's hands and a dancer's foolish neck." Holmes handed me the plate of scones, and I helped myself to gooseberry jam. "Yesterday afternoon, after you had left, I took a turn through Wyeth and Holywell streets. Torbram has indeed begun peddling those old books from Lord Mowbray's library, and has disposed of a whole box for the magnificent sum of five shillings. I paid sixpence for this, and I'm afraid I was overcharged." Holmes put his cup down and reached up to the top of the bookshelves. The volume was the thin copy of poems, with a good four square inches of its hideous purple cover cut away.

"One of the damaged volumes," I commented.

"One of the *deliberately* damaged volumes," Holmes amended. "Why slice away a few inches of the ugly paper you see before you?"

I had no answer to offer and so refilled our cups. We emptied them in brooding silence, and then Holmes said that he felt ready to make a call on Arthur Manning of Gerrard's. I of course went with him.

While we were walking down Baker Street looking

for a cab, I asked Holmes what he made of Lady Caroline's and Eustace's apparent joint disappearance.

"It concerns me," he replied seriously, "for I cannot think of anywhere they could go. Eustace, of course, could run to earth in any number of places, but where, when you are nearly penniless, do you take your sister, a young lady who is in the peculiar position of being the daughter of an earl, away from home under false pretenses, and virtually without friends?"

This was another question that I couldn't answer. Here a cab came from the direction of Oxford Street. It was not until we were seated behind the apron that I brought forth my hesitant question. "You don't suppose that Lady Caroline has gone to her husband?"

"He has not returned to that house off Rathbone Place and has not been seen in London since the day of the wedding; I've had the Irregulars watching. More, according to the telegrams I have been receiving, he is indeed in Paris. Besides, do you really think Lady Caroline would go to him, here or on the Continent?"

I did not. "How about Mrs. Marshall? Could Lady Caroline have appealed to her?"

"Mrs. Marshall is out of town and does not have any unfamiliar young lady with her. Ah, here we are at St. Paul's Churchyard."

These last words were spoken in such a quavering voice that I turned in surprise. I found Holmes's clothing now inhabited by an elderly gentleman with an irascible scowl, weakly blinking eyes, and a lop-sided droop to the mouth. He hoisted himself from the cab with infinite fussiness, and the hands that clamped onto my arm were openly trembling.

———

"Is this necessary, Holmes?" I whispered as I ostensibly supported his tottering footsteps down the narrow entrance way that leads to Gerrard's.

"I believe Mr. Manning ran from my name at the charity rooms," Holmes replied as quietly. "I do not intend giving him the opportunity to do the same now."

Gerrard's is one of those solid establishments that can afford to show little to the world. The bow-windows were furnished with much purple velvet, a single elegant candelabrum on the left, and a chaste christening mug on the right. Nor was there much more on display inside: only one glass case, holding a collection of memorial medals. Behind, a series of small rooms could be seen, rooms with deeply comfortable chairs and low tables, with heavy curtains over the windows and small lamps ready to be lit or not; here the real business of Gerrard's would be done with the highest degree of personal attention and the utmost of professional discretion.

An immaculately groomed young man had come forward from somewhere and stood awaiting our commands, not even speaking to offer his services. Holmes produced a card which named him Professor Earnest Uckridge of Cambridge, and in a shaking voice demanded to see Mr. Manning. We were quickly ushered into an office at the rear, a square room with dark-panelled walls shining richly in the light of the gas chandelier and a thick ivory-and-chocolate arabesque oriental carpet nearly covering the floor. Behind a large desk of ornately carved mahogany stood the little man with the goatee, his light-skinned face and deep-blue eyes telling of a Celtic ancestry.

"My health is no longer good," Holmes began in the querulous tone of his role, "and so I am forced to be accompanied by my medical man, Dr. Watson of the Indian service."

Manning bowed, his expression remaining perfectly tranquil. "Please be seated, gentlemen. May I offer you some refreshment? No? Then how may I serve you?"

"I want your opinion of this emerald," Holmes rejoined, taking a little box from his pocket and opening it to reveal his tie-pin. "It came to me under rather unusual circumstances, and at my age it is time to make arrangements for things of value. Your name, Mr. Manning, was given me as the foremost expert in this field."

"Whoever has said so was very kind," the little man replied with perfect courtesy, taking out a glass from a drawer and adjusting his desk lamp so that the light was concentrated on a black velvet pad. "Let me begin by saying that this stone is a very fine one."

"So I understand," Holmes replied peevishly, "but I would know more than that."

"And you shall, sir." The gemmologist was bringing his lens to bear. "The colour is excellent, Professor Uckridge, and—" Abruptly he broke off and became as still as stone himself, his grey head bent over his hands, one holding the glass, the other the tie-pin. Long he stayed so. Then he slowly put the glass down, pushed the lamp away, and returned the pin to its small box. "I believe I have the honour of addressing Mr. Sherlock Holmes," he said quietly, without looking up. "And of course Dr. Watson."

"Correct, Mr. Manning," Holmes replied in his own voice. "I see that your reputation for remembering every gem that has ever been in your hands is quite accurate."

"Certainly I know this emerald," the little man returned, his voice still low, "for my advice was sought for an appropriate gift on a certain occasion."

"Any gift from that hand would be treasured," Holmes responded, "your care added to the value. As I believe you know, Mr. Manning, I have been asked to find the amethyst that vanished so mysteriously during Lady Caroline's wedding breakfast. I understand that as soon as you learned that the stone had gone, you attempted to see the young lady, ostensibly to express your sympathy with her loss."

Holmes paused. Manning made neither answer nor move.

"You watched Mowbray House on Monday and Tuesday nights," Holmes went on, "each time remaining on the street in the bitter cold until it had become clear that your quarry was not going out. Becoming desperate, you called on Wednesday, didn't you? And were told by Rogers that Lady Caroline had gone to the Millbank charity rooms; that I have only just discovered myself by thinking to ask. You went to the charity rooms and, hearing that I was on the premises, quickly retreated. That same evening you attempted to follow Lady Caroline into Kent, learning too late that neither she nor Mr. Mowbray was on the train. Sympathy carried to this extent is rather extreme for a man in your position, don't you think?"

"What do you know of my position?" he replied with spirit, though his eyes stayed on the black velvet pad on his desk.

"I know that you recently paid far too much for a little topaz pendant that a certain merry monarch once gave to an actress named Nell."

"There you are wrong, Mr. Holmes. I paid not a

farthing more than the pendant was worth to me."

"What would you pay for the Thistle of Scotland, Mr. Manning?"

That brought the man's head up. He looked at Holmes with a level and challenging gaze. "Six thousand pounds. Tell Lady Caroline that for me."

Holmes's eyebrows had risen. "That is a considerably higher price than Mr. Stanley had arranged with the American. Why did you not make your offer first?"

"Because," Manning replied bitterly, "such as I do not belong in the world of Pall Mall and St. James's, and so do not hear the club gossip. *That* is my position, Mr. Holmes. Long before any hint of the clip's being on the market had reached me, Adolphus Stanley had completed his arrangements."

"Yet if you were willing to pay more—"

Manning interrupted with a curt shake of his head. "I knew nothing until I was asked to evaluate the clip. That put my professional reputation at stake; I could not be known to have any interest in the ornament. Nor could I refuse, for the request came to Gerrard's, and I am their employee—I may say truthfully their leading gemmologist."

"Yet now that it seems that a new buyer will ultimately be required, you would have me offer Lady Caroline six thousand pounds for a gem *she no longer has?*"

"I would," the little man said shortly.

"You have met Lady Caroline?"

The little man nodded. "I was required to be part of the legal negotiations to guarantee the ornament's authenticity and value, and there were papers for her to sign."

"Who else was there?"

"Lord Mowbray, his secretary, his lawyer, and Mr. Stanley."

"The Thistle of Scotland was displayed at these meetings?"

"Only at the first."

Holmes took the red plush jewel case out of his pocket and handed it to Manning. "What would you say as to the clip's present condition?"

As soon as Manning's eyes fell on the silver piece, he gave a start and reached for his glass. After several long moments he looked up, his expression one of deep puzzlement. "I was prepared to find the setting somewhat damaged, for one hardly expects finesse from a thief. But what has been done here..."

He paused as if to collect his thoughts. "Some small instrument has been inserted to pry up the claws and to force the calyx open, no doubt to remove the stone. Then, however, the claws have been bent down, bent farther than they originally were, and as well the filigree work has been depressed. These changes could certainly not have been made while the stone was in place, and yet why should they have been made afterward?"

Holmes reached forward and took the clip into his own hands. "I do not wish to make any actual experiments, for the exact condition of the clip may become evidence. Let us therefore suppose that I have already levered the claws and the filigree work away from the stone. While now dangerously loose, it would stay in place provided that the clip remained in a more or less horizontal position, would it not?"

Manning agreed. "The depth of the calyx would keep the stone there."

"Then suppose I wished to remove the amethyst, and was able to use only one hand and had to do the task quickly. I place my thumb at the top, and with my fingers press against the bottom of the calyx." Holmes mimicked this action without putting any weight on the clip. "The stone is larger at the top. I should thus be able to force it out, should I not?"

"It's . . . possible," Manning said cautiously.

"I would of course have pushed in the filigree work as the stone slid out. If I did not release my fingers at precisely the right moment, might I not also inadvertently press down the claws?"

Manning scowled thoughtfully, his eyes narrowed in consideration. "Certainly the silver is quite soft."

"Soft enough to be bent by a man's fingers?"

"Yes. I cannot say more, Mr. Holmes."

"Thank you." Holmes returned the clip to the case and that to his pocket. "I suppose you would not care to tell me why the Thistle of Scotland means so much to you."

"Someday I may," Manning replied, "but not at the moment. You will not take my message to Lady Caroline, will you, Mr. Holmes?"

"If I think it will serve the young lady, I will." Holmes rose. "Let us say farewell, at least for now."

There were no cabs in sight, so we started walking along St. Paul's Churchyard toward Ludgate Hill. "Have you noted, Watson," Holmes began, and his tone was unusually sombre, "that the whole reason for the Thistle of Scotland's being at Mowbray House at all was because Lady Caroline asked to wear it— first for her wedding, then for the family dinner party?"

"Surely reasonable-enough requests," I replied, "especially when these were the only opportunities she would ever have to wear her inheritance. And she has no other valuable jewellery with which to adorn herself—I certainly haven't heard that Stanley gave her anything worthy of note."

"I merely raise the point. Then consider the question of Lady Caroline's disarranged curl papers."

"That continues to puzzle me, I must admit."

"It shouldn't, for there is only one possible answer. Who but the young lady herself could have taken them out?"

"Why would she do such a thing?" I asked, bewildered.

"What other reason could there be than that she did not wish her hair to be dressed in the style her mother had decreed, in the style she wore for the dinner party? That, you'll remember, was a circle of curls, at the centre of which the clip was placed."

"Thus being less accessible to Seeton's fingers than when the clip was pinned on top of a chignon," I said slowly, hating this conclusion, yet unable to avoid it. "What, then, of that bit of sewing thread that you found on the bathroom floor? What possible part could that play?" I was attempting to use Holmes's own discovery against the theory that I could see him now forming and that I abhorred.

"The thread may well have come from fancy-work that Lady Caroline had been doing, clung to her skirts, and then fell from her clothing while she was making a last secret check of the arrangements on the top floor. When Mr. Stanley cried out that the amethyst had gone, do you remember what Lady Caroline did?"

"Nothing, just sat there. Wait: she put her hands to her face."

"And could thereby have slipped the amethyst into her mouth. If Seeton had dropped the stone into her lap, she could have hidden it under the tight cuff of her long sleeve; then, afraid she would be searched, tucked it into her cheek."

"Really, Holmes," I protested, "this is worse than Inspector Macready's idea. Why would Lady Caroline do any of this?"

"Suppose she agreed to the marriage to a virtually unknown man out of frustration with the narrow confines of her life, and then discovered that she couldn't go through with it. Unable to bring herself to face the social stigma of breaking her word, could she not have decided to make away with her own jewel in order to put the onus on Stanley to end the marriage, sure that he would do just that?"

I couldn't answer this in any way satisfactory to me.

"Think," Holmes pressed, "of the young lady as we have seen and heard of her. Think too of Manning's obvious belief that she either has the amethyst or knows where it is, and he saw her during the negotiations for the marriage, at a time when her change of mind may well have occurred."

"But what could she have done with the stone?" I asked, rather desperately. "Alone of those at the table, her person was thoroughly searched, and she surely couldn't have kept the jewel in her mouth for long."

"She could have passed it to her brother, who was not searched and would know he would not be. Who would notice or remember if, during all the confusion, he gave his sister a sympathetic embrace?"

"Even if Lady Caroline in her deep distress appealed to her brother, do you think Eustace would have the ability to plan the theft, or more knowledge of how to dispose of it afterward than Lady Caroline herself?"

"Possibly not, but Carr Fitzgerald would. Remember that the evening we saw him and that boy in the check trousers was *before* Eustace had obtained his latchkey. Also remember that we have as yet no proof that he did blackmail Seeton and Essie into providing it; they may have given him a key as part of the whole developing scheme for stealing the amethyst."

"Then the boy in the check trousers was Eustace!" I exclaimed.

"The 'boy' may have been Eustace," Holmes corrected, "disguised because he wished to take no chance of anyone's recognizing him during his meeting with Fitzgerald. The 'boy's' clumsiness, which, as you know, has steadily puzzled me, would have been caused by Eustace's unfamiliarity with the heavy boots he was wearing. Certainly he and Fitzgerald are at least acquainted: I am told that they nod when they meet at the clubs."

"Fitzgerald is certainly capable of masterminding the whole thing," I unwillingly conceded.

"And of disposing of the stone, which is a problem which has bothered me considerably. I find it hard to believe that Seeton has any contacts who would know how to do so, or who would dare even to try."

"Then after all you think Macready was right about what happened on that top floor of Mowbray House?"

"He may be right in method, yet wrong in person. Eustace, having put a sleeping drug in the cups of the guards, could have gone quietly up to that top floor and into the bathroom; if he were heard, he could always say that he was checking the alertness of the watchers. As the young master he would have a right and a presumed innocence that a footman couldn't claim. And, as Essie and Seeton both say, Eustace is already their partner in some enterprise;

perhaps he has been involved in far more than merely obtaining a latchkey."

I thought of all this and, much as I would have liked to have kept Lady Caroline's name totally free from suspicion, I had to admit to myself the strength of Holmes's reasoning. Fitzgerald to plan the deed and to dispose of the amethyst, Eustace to loosen the setting, Seeton to push the stone out and drop it into Lady Caroline's lap, she to slip it first under her cuff, then into her mouth, and finally to Eustace, who would pass it to Fitzgerald.

"It all fits," I conceded heavily.

"No, Watson," Holmes replied with unexpected vigour, "it does *not* all fit. What of those valueless books in the library whose bindings have been so deliberately cut, what of the other volumes whose covers are so curiously water-stained?"

I could find no comfort in this. "Probably of no relevance at all, Holmes."

"What of that little toy head that Lady Caroline was clutching like a life-preserver? I know, I know, you'll say that that is of no importance either. Then where did she go when she said she was leaving for the charity rooms and did not arrive there, why did she return crying, and where are she and Eustace now? And why?"

"You don't suppose Fitzgerald has anything to do with their disappearance?" I asked uneasily.

"I don't think any gentleman would introduce Carr Fitzgerald to his sister, if that is what you fear," Holmes replied drily, "no matter what the necessary business relations of the three."

More than one cab driver had looked our way during the past several minutes. We paid no heed and walked on, now in silence. At length Holmes murmured, as if to himself, "The most likely suspect of course, was..."

"Not Lady Caroline?" I asked eagerly.

"At the beginning of the case I certainly thought not. Unfortunately, so much of the evidence has since led to her."

We walked on. At length I asked, "You have heard nothing more from Inspector Macready?"

"As a matter of fact," Holmes replied disinterestedly, "he called yesterday, ostensibly because he was passing and had a spare moment. His eyes are now dark-ringed, his nails are bitten to the quick, and his manner alternates between strained bonhomie and scarcely disguised pleading. I fancy that Lord Mowbray has told his fellow peers of his dissatisfaction, they have expressed their lordly annoyance to the Home Secretary, he has informed the Chief Constable of his displeasure, that official has made his feelings known to Macready's superiors, and the inspector has accordingly been called on the carpet. Unfortunately, though the man did everything except openly beg for assistance, I had no help to offer him. I—"

"Holmes!" I grabbed his arm. "Isn't that Eustace Mowbray?"

"Where, Watson, where?"

"Just turning that corner, heading north off Cock Lane. I can't be positive," I added, "though nearly so."

These last words I had to call after him, for Holmes was already sprinting for the corner. If he hadn't been forced to pause there, I wouldn't have been able to catch him. Ahead of us was King Street, once an attractive Georgian terrace; now the frequent street lamps, left from the days of wealth, showed all too clearly that houses built for single families were the habitation of many. Not a soul was in sight.

We walked down one side and up the other, and then Holmes headed up the steps of the house nearest the corner. "Come, Watson," he called over his shoulder, "put your eminent respectability to work. We are half-pay officers looking for lodgings." He gave a business-like pull at the bell.

"Lodgings?" I echoed doubtfully, though I dutifully took up my post at his side. "I doubt there are lodgings for let on this street, Holmes."

"Nonsense, Doctor, of course there are. Did you not observe the brass plate announcing a select academy for young ladies at Number Six, the bottom of a ream stationery box covered with legal script offering to do copy work in the window of Number Three, and the ancient pram in the area of Number Two? That conjunction cries aloud of lodgings, even if Brummagem lace in the parlour and damask in the top-floor windows didn't proclaim the same."

Here the door was opened by a young maid much too small to fill her dark uniform, with her apron neither spotless nor straight, and a plump little face shiny from the heat of the kitchen.

"Good evening," Holmes began briskly. "We are looking for lodgings in this locality, and have had this house recommended by Captain Farley of the Queen's."

"Would you step in, sir, while I tells missus?" We were led through a once gracious hall now housing two large wardrobes, and left in a very small parlour, whose once no doubt grand proportions had been ruined by a wall that made architectural nonsense of the windows.

"You see, Watson?" Holmes murmured, pointing

to the jumble of photographs of military men and innumerable cheap bric-à-brac from foreign watering places that littered the mantel and several tables. "A lodging-house, a palpable lodging-house. Ah, madam, I beg your pardon for this intrusion."

The landlady was a tall, angular woman with a gimlet eye; this took on a favourable gleam at the sight of Holmes's neat person and my—as Holmes had phrased it—eminent respectability. "Jane told me that you were inquiring for lodgings," she said briskly. "I'm sorry that I can't accommodate you at the moment. Why don't you try Mrs. Robinson, two doors down? She had rooms last week, I know."

"We would prefer a house which military gentlemen frequent," Holmes replied, "for having served ourselves, we find the company of fellow officers congenial."

The woman gave a little nod of complacent agreement. "I'm partial to the military myself, sir; I always say it gives a house an *air*. You won't want Mrs. Robinson, then, for she stays pretty well with the commercials. Now let me see... You could ask at Mrs. Whitely's, just opposite. She does for officers, though her latest young gentleman doesn't have that kind of look."

"A slim young man, very fair?"

"That's the one. You know him, sir?"

"If he's the man I think," Holmes replied truthfully, "we certainly do. He wouldn't have brought his sister with him? Very quiet young lady, tall and dark. We heard that she was going to come up from the country for a few days."

The landlady shook her head. "I've not seen any sign of her, sir. But you ask at Mrs. Whitely's and see."

Back on the street Holmes paused for a moment

to inspect the house across from us. "The spare room is probably at the back. Do you stay here, Doctor, while I—"

He was interrupted by the opening of the front door and the emergence of Eustace Mowbray himself. He had changed to evening dress—his top hat with its fashionable taper from crown to curly brim was on his head, his ivory-tipped cane under his arm, he was pulling on grey gloves that appeared to match his spats exactly—and I'm not at all sure that he wasn't humming a light tune. We remained where we were, motionless in the shadow of a thick privet hedge, until Eustace had started toward Cock Lane. Then, with a few quick strides, we had our quarry cornered, Holmes at his side, I at his heels.

"Good evening, Mr. Mowbray." Holmes's tone was perfectly courteous, though his touch on the young man's arm lingered there.

If ever guilt and confusion were personified, it was by Earl Mowbray's heir. "Oh, I say," he stammered, blushing to his hat brim, "Mr. Holmes. And," with a glance of misery over his shoulder, "Dr. Watson. Oh, dammit. I mean . . ." He twirled his stick helplessly. "This is deuced awkward, don't you know."

"It is at least a little surprising," Holmes agreed, "since we have been told that you had accompanied Lady Caroline down to Kent."

Eustace nodded dejectedly. "That's where I'm supposed to be, Mr. Holmes, no doubt about that. But, dash it all, it's a living morgue down there, don't you know. And anyway," with a brief burst of determination, "I've got business to see to—urgent business —that requires my presence in London, don't you know."

"You are attempting to pay the debts you acquired during your time with the Queen's by playing cards at the clubs," Holmes calmly replied.

"Well, I must say...That is, don't you know... Well, yes. Though," Eustace added unhappily, "I'm damned if I can see how you figured it out."

"You're sharing lodgings with a friend from your regimental days?" Holmes inquired.

The young man nodded. "Trundle-bed. Pull it out at night, don't you know. I pay a bit, helps m'friend —he ain't flush with the ready, either—and all's well, don't you know. I mean to say, it *was* all well," he concluded gloomily. "Now look here, old feller," he buttonholed Holmes in sudden confidentiality, "can't we keep this mum? I mean, what's the harm?"

"Suppose you tell us just what has happened, Mr. Mowbray," Holmes suggested, disengaging his coat, "and perhaps we can leave the matter between us."

"I jolly well hope so," Eustace said fervently, "for there'll be the deuce of a row if the governor ever finds out, that I can tell you. Well, Cal got fed up with hangin' around Mowbray House—and no wonder— and said she'd rather go down to the place in Kent. Shows the poor girl's not herself, for nobody in their right mind could possibly want to go to Mowbray Park.

"The mater wouldn't hear of Cal's going alone, Will's still in gaol—which is a piece of absolute tom-foolery if you ask me, not that anyone has—so the governor told me off to take Cal down. I didn't mind that, but I was supposed to stay there, and that was the limit, don't you know. Cal knew how I felt and was sorry about it, and so, when we got to Charing Cross, she said she didn't need anyone to go with her, and why didn't I stay in London, and just keep away from Mowbray House? So that's what I've done, don't you know."

"You saw Lady Caroline onto the train?"

———

"Well, no," Eustace admitted, "she didn't want me to. 'I'm not a baby,' she said, 'for all I'm treated like one.' She had a bit of spunk about her when she said it, didn't look so much like the tag-end of a wet week, don't you know, and all she'd got with her was a small bag. So I said, 'Right you are, old girl,' and handed over the money the governor had given me for her fare—"

"No doubt keeping the money he'd given you for yours?"

"Well, yes. And've put it to good use since, believe me. Everything seemed all nice and rosy," Eustace concluded sadly, "and now this."

"Don't let our little discussion upset you," Holmes said reassuringly. "I don't think we need mention it to anyone, nor to trouble you further."

"Oh, I say!" The young man's vacant face had brightened wonderfully. "That's frightfully decent of you, I must say. Don't suppose you've found out anything useful about poor Cal's amethyst?"

"Nothing conclusive, I'm afraid."

"Well, I hope you do soon, that's all I can say," Eustace said emphatically. "That inspector feller's useless, and on Sunday that deal Stanley made with the American ends. Then what's to happen to poor Cal?"

"You don't think Lady Caroline might be better off without the marriage to Stanley?" I interjected.

Eustace looked aghast. "And stay forever down in Kent? I mean, there's not much use in her even comin' up for the season again. I mean," he lowered his voice, "it's just awful to say it right out, don't you know, but the governor's lawyers have had their eyes skinned for years, on the look-out for a marriage for Cal. That's how they knew at once that this arrangement with Stanley was the best bet they were going to find: it's that or nothing for the poor old girl. You've got to find that bally amethyst, Mr. Holmes, you've just got to. Don't you know," Eustace added.

We parted with cordial handshakes.

"Holmes," I said as we walked back down George Street, "Eustace knows nothing of his sister's present whereabouts."

"I agree with you, Doctor. More, his continuing anxiety to stay at the card tables suggests that he expects no secret windfall from the disposal of the amethyst. Or could he be playing a deeper game?"

We walked on in yet more silence. Finally I hailed a cab. As it started toward us I asked Holmes urgently, "What is the present state of the case?"

Holmes waved his stick to where on the horizon the black outline of the new Tower Bridge could just be seen. The construction on each bank was finished, and the massive girders that would complete the passage reached out toward each other like hands eager to meet. "That, Watson," Holmes said bitterly, "is the present state of the case. The structure is firmly begun, is surely nearly completed. Yet a huge gap remains to be closed, and until that is done, the whole is useless."

Chapter IX

. . . The plane tree's kind
—Edith Nesbit,
Child's Song in Spring

Holmes was just about to step into the cab when a shrill little voice came out of the dark behind us. "Mr. 'Olmes! Wait up, can't yer!" Scampering up, ragged coat flying, was Wiggins, chief of the half dozen street arabs whom Holmes had labelled his Baker Street Irregulars.

"There's somefing up at that gent's club," he reported, panting.

"You haven't left it unguarded?" Holmes asked sharply.

"Not on yer life, sir! Wotcher think I am? Muzzie is awatchin' of it. A chimbley-sweep's gorn up to the roof, but there ain't none been ordered. I knows 'coz I told the chap wiv the braid on 'is coat and 'is nose in the h'air that I was a chummy lookin' for me mahster, and I thought 'e was workin' there. 'There ain't no sweep workin' 'ere,' 'e says, 'so yer can just 'op it.' But I'd seed the sweep go up wiv me own eyes, Mr. 'Olmes, brushes under 'is arm and all, and 'is ladder's still standin' there. So I whistled up Muzzie and took off for Baker Street. Mrs. 'Udson told me yer'd gorn to Ger'ad's, and a chap outside there 'ad seen yer 'ead this way, so I followered yer. Mrs. 'Udson," he added, "said a tel'gram 'ad come for yer. A H'irish tel'gram, 'er said."

"Ah!" Holmes exclaimed. "In you get, my lad. Come, Watson." Jumping into the cab after us, he told the driver to head as fast as he could to Pall Mall. "There's only one telegram from Ireland that I'm expecting, and that concerns Fitzgerald's uncle."

"You think this means that the old man has gone?" I asked, putting a restraining arm around Wiggins, who, standing between us, was prancing with the excitement of the fast ride.

"That seems the most likely explanation." Holmes said no more until we reached the short curve of Cockspur Street. Then he leaned forward to gaze sharply out into the dark, and I had a fleeting glimpse of a couple of rangy horses moving restlessly in the shadows of the Opera Arcade.

"Bobs Gilder and one of his chums," Holmes observed. "I don't suppose you know Bobs, Doctor?" I acknowledged my ignorance. "Certainly his company is rather an acquired taste. A very neat rider, now banned from the turf for an unfortunate propensity for pulling at inopportune moments. Bengie has heard some news from Ireland too, I think, and is calling up reinforcements against an escape. Any animal Bobs has between his knees could run rings around the best cab horse in the city."

We had turned down Pall Mall when Holmes called a sharp order to halt and, telling our driver to wait, leaped out. "Stay here, Wiggins, unless you hear me whistle. Come, Doctor, though I fear we'll be too late."

———

At the back of the Traveller's, leaning against the wall, was, as Wiggins had reported, the sweep's ladder, with the faithful Muzzie lurking at the bottom.

"'E ain't come down yet, sir," he whispered.

He had to raise his tousled little head to make this report, for Holmes was already half-way up the ladder. Within seconds he had vanished into the darkness above, and Muzzie and I were left to contemplate each other and the quiet street for several minutes. I had just found a bit of toffee in my pocket and had given it to the boy when Holmes appeared at the ladder's top. His descent was considerably slower than his mounting, which in itself told of his disappointment.

"We've been nicely diddled, Watson," he said ruefully. "Our only consolation must be that Bengie and his cohorts have been as equally taken in. Fitzgerald obviously made his plans as soon as he moved to the Traveller's, discovered an access to the roof from the attic and provided himself with some disreputable garments. He then found a sweep of sturdy size who lives just off the Haymarket, and arranged that, when he received a certain message, he was to come to the club, put his ladder at the back, and go up to the roof, taking a couple of old brushes with him. He received the message over an hour ago, and found waiting for him on the roof a gentleman in wretched old clothes, who used the sweep's soot to besmear himself mightily and then calmly climbed down the ladder, old brushes under his arm. The real sweep is now sitting with his back to a chimney, enjoying a smoke with the air of a man who feels he has earned the two pound notes he now has in his pocket."

"Fitzgerald pays well," I commented.

"One of the notes," Holmes returned drily, "was mine." He put his fingers to his mouth, and in seconds Wiggins came bounding up. Holmes sent him and Muzzie to scour the area for any signs of the missing gentleman-sweep.

"They won't find anything," I said positively. "It's too dark and too late."

"You're probably quite right, Doctor, but yet we must be sure." Holmes instructed our cab driver to circle Pall Mall to Carleton Terrace, and several times jumped out to investigate some shadowed doorway or narrow entry. Wiggins made the only discovery: the two worn-out brushes, poked under a bush in the back garden of the Traveller's. At that Holmes dismissed the lads with a couple of shillings' reward each, and they scampered off, each with one of the old brushes, I've no doubt to use in some of their urchin pranks.

Holmes was far from sharing their light spirits. "Where in the name of the devil would Fitzgerald go?" he muttered with vexation, flinging himself into a corner of the cab.

"I am more concerned with the whereabouts of Lady Caroline," I said. "I am quite sure that Fitzgerald can look after himself."

"Where to, Gov'nor?" the driver called down.

Holmes paid no more attention to him than he had to me. "All the regular ports—as well as what I may call the regularly irregular ones—will be watched by Bengie's employers, both here and on the Continent, of which Fitzgerald will be well aware."

"And he is now decked out in the sooty attire of a chimney-sweep," I added. "Surely he won't go far like that."

"Certainly he needs a chance to wash thoroughly, to change into fresh clothing, possibly to collect a bag of personal items, and then, somehow, to find a way to leave London unnoticed."

"Not a small task for a man who has alert enemies everywhere. Fitzgerald must be in nearly as bad a situation as Lady Caroline."

"No, no, for, in spite of his debts, Fitzgerald still has ready money in his pockets, and as well has all the advantages of his sex. Otherwise your comparison is—" Holmes broke off and stared at me, his eyes seeming to gleam from his sudden fervour. "Watson," he cried exultantly, "you've done it. That's it—that's the answer." He jerked open the slot in the cab roof and called up to our patient driver, "Millbank Street and Horseferry Road, as fast as you can."

"Right-ee-o, Gov'nor" came back the cheerful answer, even as the cab started to roll.

"Millbank Street and Horseferry Road," I repeated. "Mrs. Marshall's charity rooms?"

"Exactly, Watson. Which, if I were the faultless reasoner you delight in depicting, I would long ago have realized."

"I still realize nothing," I said, hanging on to the side of the cab as we swung onto the Embankment.

"Come, come, Doctor. What were those charity rooms originally built for?"

"A warehouse of some kind, I should think."

"You think correctly. But warehouses line only the southern side of the street; the north is taken up by small shops. Why?"

"Well . . ." I hadn't thought of the area in this way, though I now remembered that Holmes was accurate in his summary. "The river," I said after a moment, and by then the smell of it was strong in my face. "The warehouses were built on the river for ease of shipping." I felt a surge of excitement. "And that could mean ease of escape? But there are innumerable warehouses all along the river, many of

174

them due to be torn down for the continuation of the Embankment. Why should Fitzgerald choose that particular one?"

"Can't you guess the answer, Watson?"

Then I remembered: Eustace Mowbray knew Fitzgerald and certainly knew the charity rooms, for he escorted his sister there on her weekly visits. And if Eustace had been part of the theft of the amethyst, then he had a very good reason indeed to assist Fitzgerald in his escape.

We were already in the odiferous gloom of Millbank Street, three or four scrawny cats springing out of the way of our careening cab as we rattled on. The whole area was much quieter than it had been on our daytime visit; only the old-clothes man, stooped under the pack on his back and half a dozen battered hats of different styles and sizes on his head, was in sight. Sounds there were, many and varied, but all from a distance, muffled, somewhat ominous. Except for the yellowish glow from the public house, the single eye of a crouching beast amid a jungle of unseen dangers, there was only one colour in all the area: black, in all its possible hues and variations.

At Holmes's sharp order, the cab pulled up at the top of Horseferry Road and there remained while we felt our careful way toward the water. The warehouse door was locked, but that was no problem: a moment's attention from Holmes's long-nosed pliers, and the door was open. Once this would have shocked me; now I was long used to Holmes's habit of never leaving home when on the trail of a case without a few unorthodox items stowed about his person. He cautiously stepped into the warehouse, and I as cautiously followed.

Enough light, or at least ease of darkness, came from the open door to show us the trestle-tables, bare now. In a corner stood half a dozen boxes packed with folded clothes and, nearby, a couple of barrels overflowing with a miscellany of garments apparently discarded. Much more arresting was the very faint sliver of light that showed at the bottom of the distant office door, and the low murmur of voices that came from beyond.

"Remember that small door behind Mrs. Marshall's desk?" Holmes whispered. I didn't, for in that dim and cluttered small space I hadn't noticed it. "And remember that Mrs. Marshall told the girls that after they'd finished tidying away they would have tea," Holmes added. That meant nothing to me at all, though I had no time to ask questions. Saying over his shoulder, "Very quietly, Watson," Holmes started across the worn floor.

We stopped at every creak, though I think the danger of our being heard was very slight. Not only was the rickety structure constantly emitting the moaning complaints common to old buildings, the myriad little sounds of the Thames at night drifted up from the back. As well, those who shared the warehouse with us were too deeply engrossed in their own affairs to be aware of our close proximity. Certainly we eased our way into Mrs. Marshall's office without having been discovered. A six by three foot rectangle was outlined in flickering light on the far wall, and from behind it came two voices.

"*More* hot water?" A light and laughing response from a woman in tones that I didn't recognize.

"A final rinse." A man's, also strange to me, though the faint trace of an Irish lilt to the deep baritone left little doubt. Water splashed, covering our careful approach to the plank door, unlatched and hanging crookedly on its rusty hinges. "Hand me that shirt, will you, m'dear? There, much better." An amused laugh. "Think anyone will notice a pile of sooty clothes on top of the dustbin?"

"What does it matter if they do?" Excitement and a little triumph rang through the gentle accents. "We'll be far away by dawn."

"*I*, m'dear. Not *we*. To go with me would be permanent ruin for you."

"Do you think I care? The only happy hours I've ever known in my whole life have been those I've spent with you."

"You're the only person in the world who can say that," the man replied quietly. "Let me treasure that memory unspoiled by having to think that I have at the last hurt you."

"If I only had that amethyst—"

"I would tell you to keep it."

Now with a hard push of his hand Holmes sent the ill-fitting door flying open. Before us was a small space no doubt meant as a sleeping cubicle for a night watchman. A battered iron cot, covered with half a dozen old coats, took up half the room. The only other furniture was a badly gouged deal table, which held a dusty gas ring, a kettle, a basin, and a few pieces of much-chipped crockery. Facing us were the big man we had seen near the Lyceum, his face showing the ravages which the dark had then kindly covered, and, dressed in a tweed overcoat with a deep shawl collar, Lady Caroline. Her face had been flushed with emotion; this was now draining away, and her eyes were huge and stunned.

"The tide is about to make," Holmes said quietly, "and it is certainly time Mr. Fitzgerald left. Perhaps Lady Caroline would permit us to escort her to more suitable lodgings."

For a long moment we all stared at one another. Then Lady Caroline, with a defiant lift to her head, spoke, and her flat tones made her voice once again familiar to me. "Mr. Sherlock Holmes and Dr. John Watson, Carr. My cousin, Carrington Fitzgerald."

"Cousin?" I exclaimed.

The big man gave a crooked grin. "At one time, when she was a child and I a harum-scarum boy, Caroline and I knew each other well. Lady Mowbray and my mother were sisters, you see, though it's many years since I have been welcome to call in either town or country." Reaching under the bed, he pulled out two heavy bags. "I won't pretend to understand how you gentlemen came here, but your arrival is most timely. You are quite correct: I must depart quickly, or this amusing little charade will have been for nothing."

Lady Caroline caught at his arm. "Take me with you, Carr! Don't let *them* stop you!"

"I don't, m'dear. But I won't take you."

At that she dropped his arm and stepped back, her eyes draining of life. "You don't love me, then."

"But I do, Cal. I always have, and the fact that I'll never see you again should prove it." Gently, he kissed her brow, and picking up his bags, walked by us. At the door he turned. "By the way, Cal, I've paid Eustace's debts."

"But how could you—"

"Oh, I've still some spare cash," he said with another grin, "though far from enough to satisfy my creditors. Tell Eustace to stick to the card-rooms, and he'll do well enough." With that he was gone.

Holmes at once turned to me. "Would Mrs. Watson accept Lady Caroline as a house guest for a few days, Doctor?"

"Most certainly," I replied, heartily relieved at the suggestion.

———

"You have a bag, Lady Caroline?"

Wordlessly she handed Holmes a small case from behind the table, and we left. At the outer door Holmes took out his pliers and used them to lock the warehouse; Lady Caroline gave him an appraising glance that suggested to me that Fitzgerald had entered in much the same unorthodox fashion, but said nothing. After walking up Horseferry Road, we sent our cab for a four-wheeler; while we waited we were all silent.

Once we were inside, however, and on our way toward Paddington, Lady Caroline asked the question that cried to be answered, asked in a voice taut with emotion. "Do you know where my amethyst is, Mr. Holmes?"

"I do not, Lady Caroline. *But I will.*"

"Don't find it until after Sunday!" she begged fiercely, and as we passed under a street lamp I could see her hands clasped in appeal. "Then he—Mr. Stanley—will start annulment proceedings, and all the awfulness will come to an end."

For a moment Holmes said nothing, and when he did speak his first words startled me. "Will you exchange promises with me, Lady Caroline? I will promise that, should I find your amethyst before Sunday, I will keep that fact secret for a few days."

"Oh, thank you, Mr. Holmes!"

"Wait until you hear the promise I require from you: that you tell Lord Mowbray and the countess that, regardless of whether the amethyst is found or not, you do not wish to be Mr. Stanley's wife. Otherwise you risk having the whole awfulness, as you have labelled it, repeated with some other man."

She gave a dumb nod of agreement.

"There is a second part to the promise, Lady Caro-

---

line. You told your brother that you weren't a baby, even if you were treated like one. Make that your motto. Will you?"

Slowly she reached out her hand, and Holmes touched it.

"The pact is made," he said solemnly, "and you're our witness, Doctor."

Lady Caroline looked so pathetic, sitting huddled in the corner of the cab, that I blurted out, "Why did you ever agree to the marriage with Stanley?"

"I was fool enough to think that any life would be better than the one I was leading," she replied wearily, "and, once I had given my word, and all the preparations had been made, and everyone else was so pleased, I felt I had to go on with it. At least," and here her voice trembled, "I thought that until I met Carr again."

The name seemed to have released a torrent, for the words now poured forth. "I hadn't seen him since I was a child, I didn't know he was even in England, and then last month I was with Eustace going to the charity rooms, and we saw Carr. He'd heard of my inheritance and engagement and came across to congratulate me. At least he congratulated me on the inheritance and then said, 'And you're engaged to Dolph Stanley, I hear. Are further congratulations in order, Cal?' All at once I . . . I had to talk to him. I made Eustace get out, and Carr jumped into the cab with me, and we drove . . . oh, I don't know where, and we told each other everything, as we used to do. I said Carr was better off than I, for he was a man and could at least go where he pleased, while I was a prisoner. He asked if I thought marrying Mr. Stanley would set me free, and all at once I could see what my life would be. It was like looking at an endless desert, and I started to cry.

"Carr—he never could stand tears—told me to dry my eyes, that that wouldn't help, and asked what had happened to all my daring. I felt he...he thought I'd become a weakling, just like all girls, and I said...Oh, I don't know what I said! Carr was half teasing, half scolding, and saying I'd become just like my mother, and I was denying it, and...Then I said I'd prove to him I hadn't changed: I'd go out with him that very evening. 'Done,' he said. We used to play all sorts of pranks on people, you know, dressing up and pretending to be beggars or gypsies or anything that Carr dreamt up. So I took some boys' clothes from the charity rooms, put them on, and climbed down the plane tree. When I met Carr at the corner, as we'd arranged, he laughed so much we had to jump into his cab before someone heard him.

"We went to a theatre and sat in the gallery, and to a penny gaff, and had oysters out of a stall, and drank beer in a public house, and looked at Covent Market, and...It was wonderful, wonderful! Don't look at me like that, Dr. Watson! If you knew how miserable I was, you wouldn't blame me, indeed you wouldn't. All Mr. Stanley ever seemed to think of was consols and Lombard Street and 'Change; he really didn't pay any attention to me at all, not once the papers had all been signed. I had started by being...nice to him, the way I thought I should be, and then, when I realized my terrible mistake, I...I tried to show that his company didn't please me. I thought he would be offended, you see, and...But he never seemed even to notice.

"Things just went on, there was so little time between the engagement and the wedding, and I didn't know how to stop them. Then I thought that if I asked to wear the Thistle of Scotland for my wedding, Mr. Stanley would be sure to object, and I could use that as an excuse for . . . But he agreed at once. So I asked to wear the clip for the dinner party; that was my last hope, and once more he agreed. There didn't seem to be anything else I could do."

"Did you see Fitzgerald again before your wedding?" I asked.

She shook her head.

"But you tried to, didn't you?" Holmes interposed gently. "On the night before your wedding, you took the curl papers out of your hair, put on your boy's disguise and went . . . where?"

"To Carr's lodgings. You needn't be shocked, Dr. Watson, for he wasn't there. Outside there were such strange-looking women, painted like dancing dolls and dressed very décolleté, and many of the men seemed drunk, and they were all leering at me—I don't think I fooled them for a minute with my boys' clothes. I was frightened and ran home."

"All the way?" I asked, aghast. She nodded. "Why didn't you take a cab?"

"I didn't have the money," she replied simply, and I could have cursed myself for my tactlessness. "Since the wedding," she went on, "I've thought I'd go mad waiting, that I'd go mad if the amethyst turned up. Mrs. Marshall was so sure you'd find it, Mr. Holmes; that was why I tried to avoid you, to hinder you if I could."

"When you left Mowbray House pretending to go to the charity rooms, I suppose you went again to try to see Fitzgerald?"

Once more she nodded. "But this time I had a little money for the cab, so I drove to the Haymarket and sent a boy up with a note. He came back, saying that the gentleman had moved, and no one knew where. So I had to go home. I'd have driven around all day and all night, hoping to see him, if I could. Of course I didn't have the money for that."

"Why did you say you wanted to go to Mowbray Park?"

"So I could get away without anyone's thinking about me. The river runs right behind the charity rooms, and that was . . . where I intended going."

"Lady Caroline," I interrupted firmly, but she in turn cut me off.

"Don't worry, Dr. Watson, that's all over. In fact," she gave a most dreary-sounding little laugh, "it was almost funny. When I'd sent Eustace away, I took a cab from Charing Cross to Millbank Street and walked down Horseferry Road to the wharf. I don't think I would really have jumped in, but I didn't have the choice. It was low tide, you see, hardly any water, just stinking mud. And no matter how desperate I thought I was, I wasn't fool enough to walk out into that.

"So there I stood, my bag in my hand, wondering what on earth I was going to do. Then I noticed that an old window at the back of the warehouse wasn't boarded up very tightly, and I managed to climb in. I'd thought of that gas ring in the little room where we used to make tea, and decided that if I had a cup it would help me think.

"Then I found two men's bags, with CJF in gold initials on them, pushed under the cot, and I suddenly remembered that on the night that Carr and I were together, I'd told him about my helping Mrs. Marshall, and he'd insisted on seeing the charity rooms. He left me in the cab, and when he came back he was grinning. 'Very fine quarters,' he said, 'just what the doctor ordered.' I didn't know what he meant then; now I do. He'd told me that, once his uncle had died, he was going to run off to the Continent, whether he was wealthy or penniless. I thought that if I were waiting for him, he'd take me with him. He . . . hasn't."

"Fitzgerald has for once behaved like a gentleman," I said severely.

"You would feel that way," she retorted, with just a touch of spirit.

"I'll leave you here," Holmes suddenly spoke, and I realized with a shock that we were at Baker Street. *"Au revoir,* Lady Caroline, for a few days."

"Excuse me for a moment," I said and hastily followed Holmes onto the pavement. "I can see that much has been explained by these revelations," I said in an urgent whisper. "Do you truly not know where the amethyst is?"

"I can give you my word of honour," Holmes replied bitterly, "that I am little farther on than I was last Sunday. Little farther than Inspector Macready, and how can I say more?"

With that he strode away.

Chapter X

My wife accepted her unexpected guest with the quiet equanimity that is all her own. Indeed, if anything could have eased the burden Lady Caroline carried, I think it was Mary's warm yet unobtrusive sympathy. I know that on Sunday I overheard this brief conversation between the two women.

"Did you wonder why I chose to be married in St. George's, Mrs. Watson?"

"I thought it might be because it was Little Dorrit's church."

"Exactly so. I felt rather like Little Dorrit, you see —not really orphaned, only..."

"Yes."

"I was determined to have that much romance about my wedding, for there surely didn't seem to be any other. When I told Mr. Stanley where I wanted the service to be, he said, 'Little Dorrit? Who's she? One of your relations?'"

"Oh dear!"

"Then when I explained he said, very indifferently, 'Oh, just a character in a book. All right for women, no doubt, but a man hasn't time for that kind of nonsense.' Do you know what his engagement gift was to me? A complete set of Dickens."

"That was kind of Mr. Stanley."

"In the sixpenny edition. I couldn't live with such a man, Mrs. Watson, truly I couldn't."

"Certainly not. Nor shall you."

I most fervently hoped my wife was right, but I, with Holmes, felt that Lady Caroline's freedom was going to depend upon her own powers, on what Mrs. Marshall had labelled her stock of insistence. That Holmes would ultimately find the amethyst I had no doubt, and what pressures would then be brought upon Lady Caroline to submit to either the marriage with Stanley or to some other equally distasteful to her? At least the fateful Sunday came and went with no word from Holmes, so legally the arrangement of sale with the American would have expired.

Two more days went by, and I was beginning to worry about Lady Caroline's presence under our roof. Soon, surely, there would be a letter or message of some kind from her mother to Mowbray Park, and the housekeeper, after waiting for a few days, would send word that Lady Caroline was not at her country home. Before long the police would be summoned, and Mary and I would be in a difficult situation. Wondering if Holmes could drop a word in official ears that would prevent this, on Wednesday I called at Baker Street.

I found Holmes busy at the much-scarred old table, two smoking vials adding their marks to the wood's surface, the air so thick with a mixed brew of chemicals that my first act was unceremoniously to fling open the window.

———

"One of these days, Holmes," I said severely, "you are going to asphyxiate yourself."

He gave me an amused glance. "No, no, Doctor, there is nothing here of threat to life or breath. At least not to mine, for I have hopes that a criminal or two will suffer as the result of my experiments. Have you dined?"

I had, and if I had not, the reek of that room would, I'm sure, have destroyed all hope of appetite.

"Then are you free for a walk through the heart of this great City of ours? I have a couple of minor things to show you."

"You've found the amethyst!"

"I know where it is. As I should have known much earlier. I have to admit I've been as blind as a mole."

"And that bit of thread is valueless?"

"On the contrary: it is a most vital clue—in fact, it should have pointed me in the right direction from the start."

"And those old books?"

"Not the old books, Watson. The *damage* to *some* of the old books. Another important clue, and one that I was also too blind to see."

"The alteration to the setting of the clip?"

"Quite explicable, I assure you."

I pondered for a long moment, until Holmes had donned his outer clothing and we were walking along Baker Street. I could still think of no explanation for how the amethyst could have vanished from Lady Caroline's hair while she was seated at her wedding breakfast, and said as much. "I suppose," I added, "you are not going to tell me the solution?"

"I will do better than that," Holmes replied, "I will show you what gave me the final clue. We must go to Petticoat Lane." He waved his stick at a passing cab.

"Do you remember," he resumed once we were seated inside and on our way down Oxford Street, "that you told me of a patient of yours who was sewing barrowcoats for her coming baby?" I did. "There was a clue lurking there, if I had had eyes to fathom it, for I suppose the expectant mother had made herself a special pincushion, with 'Welcome Baby' on it?"

"'Baby Dear,'" I corrected, "in cross-stitch."

"Ah! I understand that such an item is part of nearly every woman's preparations, for few will trust a safety pin near their babies and so the napkins and barrowcoats are sewn on."

I agreed, saying that many women were afraid that a pin could come undone and hurt the baby.

"A few stitches are considered both more comfortable and more secure?"

I agreed again.

"Quite so."

I looked at Holmes inquiringly, but all he would add was that he had been wandering about London, looking for new clues, and that I would now see what he had found.

We got out at the Hoop and Grapes, and there, huddled against the wall, with a furtive expression in his weak eyes and a battered tin tray around his neck, was an old man in an ancient frock-coat and battered derby. On the tray were a couple of dozen of the gutta-percha toy heads, with a faded sign on the tray front saying, "Take one home for your lad. One penny."

"Good evening, Mr. Jenkins," Holmes addressed the old fellow briskly. "How do you find trade today?"

The vendor gave a little sigh. "No better, sir, no better. The fashion's completely gone from these toys, you see, but I've not made my costs back and so am loath to give up yet. My wife says I'm a fool, and doubtless I am. Doubtless I always have been. I was an usher at one time, sir," he said to me, "I was indeed, but I wasn't in demand, and so I started a little shop. Novelties, you know. That didn't pay, and I was left with stock on my hands. So I took to the streets with a barrow and did surprisingly well. At least I did for a time. I've been—"

"Tell the gentleman about the big man and the boy," Holmes broke into this tale of woe to ask.

"The pair you asked me about, sir? They came by one evening," the old vendor turned to me, "several weeks ago. Late October it would be, for the new show at the Vic Gallery had just started, and they were laughing about it. They'd been in here," he nodded his head at the Hoop and Grapes, "and on their way out saw me in my corner. 'A souvenir,' the man called out, 'a souvenir of a most delightful evening.' And dropping a shilling on my tray he took up one of the little heads, twisted it around in his fingers—that's the fun of the toys, you know: you can press the material so that the features change— and handed it to the boy. 'Oh, Carr,' he said, laughing very much, 'Mr. Stanley doesn't look like that at all! It's not his appearance I don't like.' Then they both went away, still laughing. Why, thank you, sir, thank you."

For Holmes had dropped another shilling on his tray. "If I were you," he said seriously, "I would take your wife's advice: I think the days of sale for these toys have gone. Do you know you're the only seller of them now?"

"Am I really, sir? Just think of that! And there used to be dozens. But," with a sudden frown of doubt, "how do you know that, sir, if you don't mind my asking?"

"Because it's my business to know things that no one else is interested in," Holmes replied, smiling, and led me off down Petticoat Lane.

We passed the inevitable stalls of used clothing, shook our heads at the offers of "Velks and Wingegar," and refused to consider buying a terrier bitch even if she was guaranteed to bark only at strangers. Once when we were pushing through the crowd gathered around a barrel organ, with a red-capped monkey prancing on the top, I think Holmes saved my pockets, for he suddenly clapped his hands like a thunderbolt. Wheeling around, I saw a ragged youngster dodging away through the crowd like a greased eel.

On the far side of Petticoat Lane, with his barrow pushed into a commodious corner of Commercial Road, was a ginger-beer vendor. His fancily corrugated metal urn, with a shining brass dome on top and a tap at the side, was adorned with a sign proclaiming it "The Best Drink Out," and a basket below held a tray of glasses and a pail of water for the constant washing up. A further sign on the end of the barrow promised "Ice in Every Glass" and announced the price as Only "1/2 d. a Glass." I could note nothing remarkable in the whole contraption, nor in the shrivelled shrimp of a man who was its proprietor.

"You see, Watson?" Holmes said, pointing at the sign. "The keystone of the whole structure."

This meant nothing to me at all. "Does anyone really want ice in this weather?" I asked with a shiver.

"The young 'uns do, sir," the little man replied. "Not 'aving it at 'ome, you see, it's a novelty, like. Care to try a glass, sir?"

"No indeed," I said emphatically.

"You should," Holmes said, his eyes dancing. "Consider this." And he pointed to the sign at the other end of the barrow, declaring that we had before us the "Fountain of Youth." "Still not tempted? Then let us find a cab, for Petticoat Lane has no more revelations for us."

While we were on our way back to Baker Street, I said, in a remonstrative tone, "All this is very well, no doubt, Holmes, but I don't know what you find remarkable in ginger-beer, and I am concerned for Lady Caroline."

"I haven't forgotten her, I assure you. Let another day go by, and then bring her to Mowbray House. Could you manage around eleven in the morning?"

"I could. I will."

"And, Watson, put your revolver in your pocket. I'm sure it will not be needed, but the threat of it could be useful. It will be better to leave official authority on the outside, and we should take a few simple precautions." As he left the cab he called back, "You really should have had a glass of that ginger-beer, Doctor. The best drink out, I assure you!"

Lady Caroline and I were prompt in meeting the engagement at Mowbray House. The poor young lady was very white and very quiet as she mounted the steps of her home, and who could blame her? Rogers opened the door, and as he showed no surprise at seeing his young mistress again, it was evident that he had been told to expect us. We were shown up to the grand and gloomy drawing-room where, as Rogers said, Lord Mowbray, the countess, and "a few others" already were. We found these to be Eustace, Torbram, Miss Powle, Mr. Manning, Griffiths, and Holmes.

"Excellent!" he cried, jumping to his feet at the

sight of us. "Now we can begin my little demonstration." He turned to Lady Caroline. "Before you left here for the wedding service, Miss Powle fastened the amethyst clip in your hair. May I ask her to do so again?"

Holmes had taken the red plush case out of his pocket and now opened it. There was a general cry of astonishment.

"You've found the amethyst!" Miss Powle exclaimed, waving her plump little hands in delight.

Certainly there on the scarlet silk was the silver thistle clip, with a rich purple stone sparkling at its head.

"No, don't trouble with examining the clip now, Lady Caroline," Holmes said firmly. "Allow Miss Powle to put it in your hair. Splendid. The clip looks lovely, does it not?" We all, truthfully, agreed. "I have asked," Holmes went on, "that the dining-room furniture be arranged as it was for the wedding breakfast, and, as we will be at the table for some time, the countess has kindly offered to have refreshments served. Since Mr. Stanley is not here, will you accept my arm, Lady Caroline?" She did so in stunned silence. "Mr. Mowbray, you will follow as you did on Sunday morning with Miss Powle, then Lord and Lady Mowbray. Watson, you, Mr. Manning, Mr. Torbram, and Mr. Griffiths will have to impersonate the rest of the guests."

We all did as instructed, though Griffiths whispered to me on the way down that it was a "rum go," which I certainly couldn't deny. What I was sure about was that the amethyst was glittering in Lady Caroline's hair every step of the way.

Once in the dining-room, where I was glad to see a fire was burning warmly, we sat around the table, Lady Caroline and Holmes in the centre, flanked by

Mr. Mowbray and Miss Powle and then Lord Mowbray and the countess. Manning, Torbram, Griffiths and I were across from them. The countess rang the bell, and, as Rogers poured wine, Will Seeton came in with plates of sandwiches. He had had his hair cut and his beard shaved and was of course in a neat clean uniform, but there was a sullen set to his shoulders that hadn't been there before. It would take more than Rogers, I thought, to keep that boy in service much longer.

I cannot say that any of us were in a talkative mood, but Holmes seemed determined that we should all join in conversation. He drew out Lord Mowbray on the subject of the wine, and Eustace on the revival of *The Mikado,* which had recently opened. Holmes had some intelligent questions to ask the countess about tapestry work, and she, to my surprise, was quite knowledgeable on the subject. Before I think Lady Caroline was aware of it, she was discussing Dickens with Holmes, and Miss Powle blushingly gave her opinion of *King Solomon's Mines,* which she had recently read. Torbram became almost excited on the *Dictionary of National Biography,* calling it a monumental work, Griffiths gave an anecdote from his years of police work, and I dutifully followed with one from the life of a medical man. Before I had realized it, the plates and glasses were empty, Rogers and Seeton were serving coffee, and an hour and a half had gone by.

Then Holmes rose, full wineglass in hand and every eye on him. "At the end of the wedding breakfast," he began, "Mr. Stanley got to his feet to return the toast to the bride. He looked down toward Lady Caroline," Holmes was suiting his actions to the words, "could see the hair clip but not the amethyst, and, leaning closer, spilled a little wine over the

193

bride." We all watched, mesmerized, as the drops fell from Holmes's glass onto her hair and shoulder. "No, don't look at me Lady Caroline; look away, as you did that morning. The amethyst had vanished, and Mr. Stanley cried out, 'It's gone!' As, you'll notice, it once again has."

There was a moment's paralyzed silence, then an outbreak of noisy consternation. We were all on our feet in seconds and clustered around Lady Caroline. She sat, as she had on her wedding day, stunned and motionless. The silver clip shining against her dark hair was empty.

"You got some of your wine on the clip, Mr. Holmes," Eustace observed in his fatuous way, "just like Stanley did. I wiped it up."

"Did you, Mr. Mowbray?" I could see the sharpening interest in Holmes's face. "When?"

"While we were all gathered 'round, sayin' 'My goodness' and 'Where's it gone?' and such forth. I had my napkin in my hand, don't you know, and while I was sort of pattin' Cal on the back I did this." Eustace gently dabbed his napkin to the clip. "Stanley had wiped her gown, but he hadn't noticed the clip was wet too."

"No, he wouldn't," Holmes agreed, and I could hear the immense satisfaction in his voice, "for out of courtesy to the occasion he was not wearing his spectacles. Now if you will all take your places again, I will explain the little mystery."

The rest of us obeyed, Lord Mowbray did not. "Look here, Mr. Holmes," he demanded truculently, "do you or do you not know where that damned amethyst is?"

"I do," Holmes replied calmly, "within a foot or so."

A foot or so! Whatever did that mean? I saw the same bewilderment all around me.

"Where is it?" Lord Mowbray barked furiously. "Is it in the house?"

"At the moment it is," Holmes answered, "though it has not been for all of the hours since the breakfast. If you will sit down, Lord Mowbray, we will proceed." Holmes had his way: Lord Mowbray, though scowling, sat down.

"From the beginning of the case," Holmes began, "there seemed to be two related problems. All witnesses agreed that the amethyst was in the clip, and the clip in Lady Caroline's hair, when she took her seat at the table. An hour and a half later, since the stone had apparently fallen out, it seemed that it must have been perilously loose in its setting."

"Not when it left my hands," the gemmologist interjected firmly. "That I will swear to."

"I am sure you are quite correct, Mr. Manning," Holmes responded, "for on the evening before the wedding the Thistle of Scotland was closely examined and much admired by several people, and nothing untoward was found then. Was it then possible that the amethyst had somehow been loosened during the night? This possibility was strengthened by the fact that a sleeping drug was induced into the lunch that had been prepared for the two guards, Mr. Torbram and Mr. Griffiths."

Next to me Griffiths sat up with a jerk, his eyes bulging and his mouth popping open. Someone else at the table had given a slight start, a movement that had been nearly instantly suppressed. Who it was I didn't know, but I was positive it had occurred.

"However," Holmes continued, "even if we suppose that during the night the setting had become damaged so that the amethyst fell out during the wedding breakfast, we are still left with the second problem: what happened to it then?

"From the beginning of the case Inspector Macready felt that the thief had to be someone who had no interest in the marriage. With some of the inspector's ideas I did not agree; with this I did. Unfortunately for the progress of the investigation, two other mysteries were woven around the central one." Eustace's mouth tightened a trifle, and a slight flush touched Lady Caroline's face, though I think that I was the only one to notice either. "Once these subsidiary puzzles were solved, the remaining problem became much clearer. Especially as three clues had emerged."

Holmes here turned to the butler. "We'll have the box now, if you please." Rogers left the room, and Holmes continued.

"The first clue was the particular way in which the setting of the clip had been altered. In order to have removed the stone, the thief would naturally have had to lift the little claws and the filigree calyx that held the stone in place, and there were signs that this had indeed been done. What had also occurred, though, was that the claws were bent down sharply and the calyx squashed in a way that would have been quite impossible while the stone was in place."

"Why should any thief do that?" Eustace inquired. "Senseless, don't you know. I mean to say, even I wouldn't—"

"Eustace!" his father roared, and the young man subsided.

"The second clue," Holmes resumed, "was also damage, though of a different kind. A number of books in the library had had from two to four inches of their covers cut away."

"Some of the older books are in very poor condition," Torbram interjected, "and the covers are quite brittle."

"These particular books," Holmes replied, "are not all especially old, nor are the bindings of all in poor condition. One might have been damaged in some meaningless fashion, but that seven should have suffered was very strange indeed. As well, a number of other books had faint discolorations on their bindings, rather like water stains. Ah, here is Rogers with my little box."

The butler had entered carrying a metal container perhaps four inches by seven or eight. Holmes took the box in his hand and lifted the lid so that we could all see the contents. Gasps of wonder rose around the table, for the whole bottom of the box seemed covered with amethysts, ranging in colour from a pinkish mauve to a deep purple. Then Holmes abruptly tipped the box upside down over a plate that had held sandwiches. It was into a stunned silence that Miss Powle said wonderingly, "Why, they're just bits of ice! Coloured ice."

Holmes smiled down at her. "Exactly, Miss Powle. Ice made from water that was dyed by pieces cut from the bindings of those old books, which, I suddenly realized, were all shades of blue, red, or purple. Our thief had taken a wet cloth and first tested the colours of books with such covers; some were fast, seven were not. From these last he cut the small sections of the bindings and made his dye. I'm afraid, Lord Mowbray, that I have had to damage the books a little more in order to create my own fakes," Holmes poked a finger at the plate of purplish ice, "and, as I have never seen the Thistle of Scotland complete with the stone, I have had to rely on Mr. Manning to choose from my collection the bit of ice that best matched the colour of the amethyst. Since we succeeded in deceiving you—all but one of you, that is—I think we must judge his eye as accurate."

"But I don't understand!" the countess cried. "What happened to Caroline's amethyst? It was in her hair just an hour or so ago—"

"It wasn't, my lady," Holmes corrected, "any more than it was when she sat down to her wedding breakfast. In each case a piece of ice had been put in the place of the stone, with the setting crushed down to hold it tightly, the claws and the filigree biting into the ice so that it would remain in place as it began to melt. Since Lady Caroline was then seated as she has been today, with her back to the fire, the ice turned to water and the water evaporated. There may have been a little moisture left when the inspector first saw the clip, but if he noticed anything it would be put down to the wine that Stanley spilled. If Mr. Eustace hadn't helpfully tried to wipe up that wine, would an undue trace of wetness have been found? Who can tell?"

"You mean to say," Eustace said slowly, frowning with the effort, "that somebody drugged Torbram and the guard chappie so's he could sneak into that old bathroom, open the jewel box—by the way, wasn't it locked?"

"It was, Mr. Mowbray, but finding a key to fit wasn't at all difficult."

"Really? Wouldn't have thought of that, myself. So the thief opened the box, took out the clip, forced out the amethyst, put in a bit of ice, squished the setting down tight, put the clip back in the box—"

"I don't think so, Mr. Mowbray. Since it was essential that the ice not melt too soon, I think the clip was put into the mouth of the vent that leads to the

198

roof; that was so cold that the small pool of water that had dripped down was frozen solid. That was one of the two reasons the old bathroom was chosen as the place of security over the lumber room next door; the other was that the bathroom could be visited without rousing any suspicion."

"Only by Mr. Torbram and the police chappie," Eustace broke in. "I mean—"

"You are quite correct, Mr. Mowbray."

Holmes said no more. I understood him, at last. I wonder how many others did.

Certainly Lord Mowbray did not. "All right!" he suddenly shouted, heaving himself to his feet. "All this is very clever, no doubt. What I want to know is *where that damn stone is?* How many times do I have to ask?"

"No more, I hope," Holmes replied. He waited, as did we all. No one moved. "May I point out," his voice was very quiet, "that there is no possibility of escape? You are hopelessly outnumbered." At a slight gesture from his hand, Rogers and Seeton silently took up places by the two doors.

Still the seconds ticked away, and then, white as a ghost, Torbram slowly got to his feet, and, with awkward fingers unbuttoned his coat. There, in an inside pocket, was a slight bulge.

"The amethyst," Holmes explained, "is tied in a small piece of cloth and secured by several stitches, during the day in a coat, later in a nightshirt. My third clue, you see, was a small piece of white thread that I found on the bathroom floor."

With a sudden vicious tug Torbram yanked from his pocket a tiny bundle of white and flung it onto the table.

"Arrest him!" Lord Mowbray yelled at Griffiths,

and I clapped my hand to the revolver in my coat.

"I can't arrest anyone, sir," Griffiths protested. "I'm retired from the force now."

"Then get someone who can, damn you!"

"No!" The voice was so firm, the tone so crisp that for a moment I hardly recognized it as Lady Caroline's. She was gazing at her father with level eyes and lifted chin. "Do you want the details of the trial on all the front pages of London? With no doubt some mention of Mr. Stanley's abrupt flight to the Continent?"

"Heaven forbid!" the countess cried, her face blanching.

Lord Mowbray, looking black as thunder, snatched up the little cloth package, ripped it open, and tossed the glowing purple stone to Mr. Manning. "This all right?" he demanded. Taking out a pocket glass, the gemmologist made a quick examination and then gave a short nod. "All right," Lord Mowbray snapped at his secretary, still standing by his chair, mute and with bowed head, "if you're not out of this house in half an hour, I call the police and be damned to the papers."

Silently, Torbram went. When he reached the door he half turned and, without raising his eyes, made a half-bow toward Lady Caroline. Then he had gone.

"Rogers," Lord Mowbray had the amethyst clutched in his fingers, "wire Stanley. Probably not too late—"

"No." Again it was Lady Caroline who spoke, in a voice as hard as ice and quite as cold. "Let the marriage be annulled, Father, for I will never live with Adolphus Stanley."

"Caroline!" gasped her mother. "You don't know what you're saying!"

———

200

"Yes, I do, Mama. And I know what I'm going to do too."

"What?" inquired Eustace, looking genuinely interested.

"Open a tea-shop."

"Like Buszard's?" Eustace asked, over the cry of the countess and the wordless bellow of Lord Mowbray. "Jolly good cakes they have."

Lady Caroline smiled at him. "My establishment will be much smaller than Buszard's, but I hope you'll find my cakes jolly good too."

"Well, I'll certainly give them a try, old girl."

"Eustace!"

"Well, I mean to say—"

"Caroline, have you taken leave of your senses?" her outraged father demanded. "Leaving everything else aside, you know nothing about running a tea-shop."

"I know precisely that much, Father: that I have much to learn. I am going to live with Mrs. Marshall, and she has found a tea-shop that will let me work there."

"Let you work!" her mother moaned.

"To learn, Mama. Probably once I have my own shop, I could hire Essie and Will. They're going to be getting married, Essie tells me, so they won't be able to stay in service, will they?"

"Caroline," Lord Mowbray said, in a voice hoarse with rage, "you cannot do this. I won't permit it."

"You can't stop me, Father, though I hope the time will come when you will give me your approval. I am of legal age, and the amethyst is mine. For four thousand pounds—"

"If I may be allowed to make the offer, my lady," Mr. Manning interjected, "I have a buyer who will give six thousand pounds for the Thistle of Scotland."

"Then he shall have it." Rising, she lifted the stone from her father's lifeless hand. "Rogers, send for the lawyer. We might as well make the arrangements now."

Rogers looked toward Lord Mowbray. Reluctantly he gave a short nod. "Do what you like," he muttered. "Wash my hands of the whole thing. Mr. Holmes, my thanks. Not your fault this girl is acting like a lunatic." Marching to the door, he tossed over his shoulder his final word. "Going to my club." He went out and very nearly slammed the door behind him.

Holmes and I quickly made our farewells. We received a charming smile from Lady Caroline, the wish to be remembered to Mary, and the promise that all three of us would have free tea and cakes forever at her shop. While Holmes and I were putting on our coats in the hall, Mr. Manning slipped out to us.

"Lady Caroline has thanked you," he said softly. "How can I?"

"I cannot see that you have much cause, Mr. Manning," Holmes replied, "but if you wish to let me claim a reward, tell us why the amethyst clip means so much to you."

"Because," he replied simply, "I am a descendant of Lord Darnley and the Queen of Scots. I know! It seems impossible, doesn't it? The story has long been a legend in our family, I have had it investigated, and my branch does indeed come from James the Sixth of Scotland. An illegitimate liaison, of course, yet the blood of the Stuarts runs in my veins. I know you think I'm mad to make so much of it," he added with a deprecating little smile.

"Not at all, Mr. Manning. If your hobby gives you pleasure, why shouldn't you indulge it? I should have guessed," Holmes added, pulling on his gloves, "for you collect only jewels that are connected with the Stuarts, don't you?"

"Quite correct, Mr. Holmes. Never before have I been able to acquire a stone that had belonged to one of the major members, and to have the Thistle of Scotland fulfills my wildest dreams. Be sure that if I can ever assist Lady Caroline in her business venture—my advice might be of some help to her—I will ever be at her service."

As Holmes and I stepped out of the house, a figure moved hesitantly from the shadows of the hedge.

"Should I go in yet, Mr. Holmes?"

The obsequious tones were a better disguise than the dark. It was only with difficulty that I recognized Inspector Macready.

"Your timing is perfect, Inspector," Holmes replied. "You have no arrest to make—"

"No arrest! But you assured me the case was over!"

"The disappearance of the amethyst was in the nature of a household prank," Holmes said smoothly and with little truth, "and as the stone has been recovered, there will of course be no prosecution, and hence no arrest. You will be needed, however, to escort Mr. Manning and the Thistle of Scotland, which has again been entrusted to his care, back to Gerrard's. Lord Mowbray will be sending a note to the Home Secretary, expressing his complete satisfaction with the conclusion of the case, and will mention favourably your zealous conduct."

We left a very grateful and much chastened young officer to climb the steps of Mowbray house.

"Do you think Lord Mowbray will agree to send

such a note?" I asked as we started down Mowbray Crescent.

"As I shall make it part of my fee, I am sure he will. Macready behaved like a fool, but he has at least imagination. Castor oil!" Holmes indulged in one of his soundless laughs.

"When did you first suspect Torbram?" I asked.

"From the beginning," Holmes replied to my surprise. "As Griffiths rightly said, those arrangements for guarding the clip were absurdly complex and largely pointless. I could not believe that a man as intelligent as Torbram had concocted them, and yet, in such a household, it was obviously he who would have had to make and implement the plan. Then there was his position in the house: he wasn't family, yet he wasn't quite a servant. This meant that his person wouldn't be searched, nor would the police easily suspect him: the footman certainly, but not my lord's secretary."

"I suppose Torbram chose Griffiths to be his fellow guard, and did so because he knew the man would welcome a lunch?"

"And would consume his food so eagerly that he wouldn't notice a trace of bitterness in his coffee. Certainly Torbram deliberately positioned himself next to the bathroom door for ease of access to the room."

"Did he really hear anything during the night?"

"If he did, it was Griffiths' snores. I suspect that when the old chap was on the point of waking, Torbram thought that he'd muddy the waters a little by pretending to have heard a creaking board. It would do him no harm and might produce further camouflage for him."

"Torbram of course had a good eye for colour," I mused, remembering his comments on the paintings in Mowbray House, "and with his spectacles his sight was good."

"True. Also he would have genuine understanding of how poorly someone who should wear glasses can see without them; Eustace was the only real threat, and he indeed saw accurately. He said the amethyst looked like a drop of pink champagne: the ice was beginning to melt."

"What would Torbram have done if the night's weather had turned mild?"

"His plan did not depend upon the weather, though it was aided by the cold. Remember the ice-pudding that was part of the breakfast menu? The cook would have made that with salt and ice shaved from a block. If necessary, Torbram would have sneaked down to the pantry and obtained some."

Here we found a cab and eventually parted with cordial farewells, and I hurried home to relate the day's events to my enthralled wife. When I had finished, she sat back, a smile on her lips, and said, "Do you know, John, the motto of the Queen of Scots?" I didn't. "'In the end is my beginning.' I think the same can be said of Lady Caroline."

As usual, my wife has proved quite right.

Printed in the United States
2426

9 780743 205528